THE CHRONICLES OF

JOYA

Liane Carter

Cover design by
Gwyneth and Harry Ashcroft

Lauren

Good luck with your
writing :)

Happy reading!

Liane
xo

To Renni Browne, for telling me I was born to write and for showing me how.

Maya Council

1st Seat	Hi Brid	man
2nd Seat	Darcy Maya	dog
3rd Seat	Malcolm	man
4th Seat	Professor Danny Loco	boy
5th Seat	Freddie Maya	ferret
6th Seat	Lickety Split Maya	girl
7th Seat	Zeus	boy
8th Seat	Dictionary Boy	boy
9th Seat	Estefania Maya	cat
10th Seat	Wild Bill Ferret	ferret
11th Seat	Cool T	man

This first book of chronicles talks of all council members except the 9th and 10th Seats. Look out for them in book 2.

Pronunciation

JOYA is pronounced "hoy ya"

Magi Pods are pronounced "madgy"

Maya is pronounced "my ya"

To any government official: this is purely a work of fiction.

Chapter 1

Teal struggled towards the cave door, practically dragging her dad along the floor. His teeth clung to her cottontail.

"Dad, get *off* me!"

He released his jaws and spat out some fluff. Teal dashed across the sitting room, but he bolted in front of her. He sat up on his hind legs and leaned against the door.

"You're not doing it."

"Dad, please." Teal shot a glance at the clock above the door. Her dad folded his arms across his chest.

"Teal, there's a reason why there are no rabbit Switchers. Do you—"

"Darcy Maya isn't racist when it comes to rabbits, and *she* isn't scared."

"I wouldn't be scared either if I was a great Doberman and Second Seat on the Maya Council."

Her dad's white fur twitched and his black eyes glistened. Teal looked like a smaller model, but he said she had the spirit of her mother. He never meant it as a compliment.

"I could be down on Earth helping people. You should be proud."

"Your mother got shot there. You think I want to lose you, too?"

7

"I'm not her. I've been trained."

"Against earthie dogs? Earthie humans? They're hunters down there. They hunt *us*."

Teal sighed. Her dad was happy with his life on Joya, but she wanted more. She wanted to fly right off this red and purple planet and explore the huge colourful earth Freddie Maya sang about. She'd worked her paws off for months to get down there.

"Darcy wouldn't train me if she didn't think I'd be safe," she said.

"She can't train you if you don't turn up, can she? I'll guard this door day and night if I have to. You're not going."

Teal glared at him. "You wouldn't even know if Brian hadn't blabbed."

"You'd do well to be more like him. Your cousin doesn't betray his father."

Yeah, right. Honest Brian had been sneaking off to Switcher training with Teal every morning for months, until he got thrown out of the program a week ago for cheating in an exam. Brian had known she had a shot and waited until the last day to ruin it. Teal wanted to sink her teeth into his floppy ears.

"It's what I've wanted my whole life, Dad. Please, just—"

"How many times do I have to say it? You're *not* going."

She heard the distant sound of the last horn for trainees. Even if you had a paw falling off or blood spurting out from a major vein, you still went to Switcher training. To miss the last horn meant automatic failure. In Darcy's mind, lateness showed disrespect.

"You have your whole life ahead of you, Teal. I know it seems important now, but—"

"Don't you get it? I'm dying in here, I want to make something of myself, get away from the caves. I could be the first rabbit Switcher, the first ever. I hate it here. I HATE YOU!"

Teal threw herself to the floor and sobbed. Tears soaked her fur.

She heard a creak, wiped her paws across her face, and looked up. Her dad had opened the door and stepped aside.

Teal looked at him. The expression on her father's face made her heart sink. How could she have said it?

"Dad, I …" She sniffed, went to him, and put her paw on his arm. He pushed it away.

"Let the great Darcy Maya protect you."

Teal's heart shrivelled under his glare.

"Go on. Get out."

Her dad slammed the door behind her. She looked over her shoulder. In one morning she hadn't just lost her chance to become a Switcher, she'd lost her dad, too.

She dragged herself from the cave. She walked along the red sandy trail, kicking dust into the purple fields on either side. Her dad's words from years ago filled her mind, "The red paths of Joya get darker towards the caves, so you can always find your way home, Teal."

She struck out at the red sand and it flew up in her face. She coughed, shook her head, and dug a paw in her ear to scrape the sand out. She walked on, muttering under her breath.

The Lilac Mountains stood in the distance. To climb one had been her dream once. The first time she reached the top she had sat back on her haunches, puffed out her chest, and beamed at the beauty of the planet. When had it stopped seeming beautiful to her?

Teal heard an engine and looked up in the sky. Oh, no. Freddie Maya, Fifth Seat on the Maya Council, was flying straight towards her on his custom-made red and black Harley Sportster. She looked around at nothing but open purple fields.

Teal bit her lip and thanked the Great Eagles Darcy hadn't come in person.

Freddie landed. He pressed a switch, and the stabiliser shot out. He jumped off the bike, brushed down the fur on his arms, and strutted over to Teal.

A chocolate brown ferret, Freddie Maya always wore shades over his red eyes. His headphones never left his ears, some Mayas said he even showered in them. Freddie had been a cave dweller, and look what *he* had accomplished. Number one in the Joya charts, Freddie's rap music was better than anyone's.

"What are you thinking, man?" Freddie asked. "Darcy's doing her crunch over at the Switcher Centre."

"No point going in just to be told to go home."

"You gotta learn some respect, girl. Don't be dissin' Darcy. She can be a mean ole dawg."

"It's not my fault my dad found out, Brian ratted me out. Dad wouldn't let me leave the cave and we had a fight and I told him I hated him and now he's thrown me out and he doesn't want me."

Freddie let out a whistle.

"You swing for the fence, don't you, girl?"

Teal buried her chin.

Freddie strutted back to the Harley. He ran up the side and started the engine.

"Come on, man," he said.

"What?"

"Exit interview? You have to face her. If you want to walk, it's your loss, man."

Teal's eyes lit up. A chance to fly on a Maya Council motorbike, although in her best dreams she flew a rocket.

"Hop up this way, or you'll burn up your paws on the pipes." Freddie flicked his head. "I rushed off with no helmets, so no grassing me up."

Teal nodded and jumped onto the bike. She felt *tall*. The deep sound of the engine filled her ears and vibrated through her body. They rushed into the air so fast her stomach flipped. The thrill made her fur tingle and her heart soar.

"Yee-hah!" she yelled. Freddie laughed.

As they flew over the Lilac Mountains, the wind blew on her cheeks. She looked down on the immense vivid green Unfathomable Lake.

Teal thought of Brian's dare—she'd had to swim the length of the lake balancing a Maya penny on her nose. The long black eels—caught up in her excitement—pulled her by the forepaws when Brian couldn't see. Teal chuckled.

Freddie started his descent. The white light beamed up at them: the giant crystal eye in the top of the Switcher Centre received and reflected light. It served as the only window in the deep red wooden dome, the size of all the caves put together.

Teal couldn't see Darcy's motorbike out in front with the other vehicles. Maybe she'd been called away and someone else would do the exit interview.

Freddie landed. He rode around the back of the dome and parked next to a familiar blue mud-splattered motorbike. Teal's stomach churned and her legs shook as she followed Freddie around to the Switcher Centre's gold door. Freddie placed a paw on the lowest of the three embossed silver eagles. The door opened and they walked into the circular entrance hall.

Freddie told her to wait and knocked on Darcy's office door.

"What?" Darcy said.

Freddie looked over his shoulder at Teal, took off his shades, and raised his eyebrows. Teal gulped. Freddie pushed the door and went in. Teal bit her cheek and looked down at the floor tiles.

The door slammed shut. Teal jumped. Her eyes darted between Darcy's door and the front door. No choice. She looked up at the mural on the ceiling and thought of all the past and present Switchers.

Freddie came out into the hall and shook his head.

"Good luck, man."

Teal's paw felt as heavy as a tree as she knocked on the door.

"Get in here," Darcy said.

Teal dragged herself inside and made herself look up. Her very own firing squad: a man, a boy and a Doberman. Teal had never wanted to see a fellow rabbit so much in her life.

The three of them sat behind the great red desk. Darcy, in the centre, looked regal and proud. Her black fur gleamed over her muscular body as usual, but her brown eyes seemed to pierce straight through Teal's skull. She bared her teeth and growled. Teal winced.

To Darcy's right sat Zeus, Seventh Seat on the Maya Council. A teenager like Teal except he'd become a Switcher on his fifth birthday, not just the youngest human Switcher, the youngest Switcher full stop. He pushed his black hair out of his blue eyes and pursed his lips.

On Darcy's left sat the immense boxing trainer Rocket Ron Johnson. Big, black, solid muscle, good-looking for a human— Rocket Ron had a big female following. He had no patience for Teal in the gym, so she doubted he'd go easy on her. Her eyes fell to the floor.

"Have you any idea how difficult it's been to get rabbits approved for the training programme?"

Teal looked up at Darcy, gulped, and nodded. Cats, dogs, ferrets, and humans. That's how it had been forever. Teal hadn't slept for three days when the posters went up for rabbit recruits.

Darcy closed her eyes and shook her head. She turned to Zeus and nodded.

Teal knew Zeus liked her and hoped he would say something positive.

He cleared his throat.

"Hours wasted: two-hundred and twenty. Cost: incalculable. Trouble caused: considerable. Damage to property: three chairs. Patience with fellow trainees: sub-standard. Attendance: failure to show on last day ..."

Teal's ears flopped. She must have been crazy to think she had a chance. She thought she'd done so well. She—

"Any comments, Trainee?" Darcy said.

Teal shook her head. She had prepared to explain the situation with her dad and shout out about injustice, but hearing Zeus she knew she didn't deserve to be a Switcher. She wished she could turn back the clock and undo what she'd said to her dad. What a fool she had been to think they would choose her.

Darcy let out a sigh. "Very well. Rocket Ron?"

"This trainee," Rocket Ron said, "is incapable of taking responsibility for her actions, blames others, doesn't listen,"

Teal's cheeks burned, her body slumped, and her mind screamed "stop." Rocket Ron kept going.

"She's stubborn, has no time for other trainees who don't show commitment to the course, loses patience with those who don't keep or stay at her pace, and hogs the boxing bag. She shouldn't be exited from the programme."

Teal waggled her head, stuck a paw in her ear. Did he just say *shouldn't*?

Rocket Ron smirked. "I've been hard on Teal throughout training, much harder than the others—as you requested, Darcy."

Thanks, Darcy. Blimey, and Dad thought you could protect me.

"I've been testing what this rabbit can take, and it's a lot," Rocket Ron said. "She may be stubborn, but I kind of like that." He winked at Teal and she nearly fainted. She had no idea Rocket Ron had any emotion other than anger. "She's tough, punches like a demon, moves fast, and is driven."

Teal looked open-mouthed from Darcy to Rocket Ron and back to Darcy, who stared at the boxing trainer.

Darcy shook out her fur and turned back to Teal.

"Go outside, Trainee, so we can talk about you."

Subtle. She nodded, shut the door behind her, and heard Darcy's roar from the other side.

"So you change your mind at the last minute? Teal broke Rule Number One and didn't even plan to come in and explain. No respect whatsoever."

Teal, alone in the circular hall surrounded by doors, covered her ears with her paws. She didn't mean to disrespect Darcy. She didn't think. Story of her life, her dad always said. Her dad. She thumped her forehead.

And what about Zeus, her role model Switcher? It hurt to hear the cold statistics from him. She had wanted Darcy and Zeus to be proud.

What about Rocket Ron Johnson, though? She shook her head and bit her bottom lip. Sure, he said some bad things, but didn't he always about everyone?

She straightened her back, puffed out her chest, and swayed her head from side to side. "Hi, I'm Teal. Rocket Ron says I punch like a demon." Maybe, just maybe, they might let her stay.

Darcy called her back in.

"Rocket Ron got a bit carried away," Darcy said.

"Oh." Teal's body deflated.

"I told him to be tough with you and all rabbit trainees. It seems I forgot how literal a man he is. It appears you've had more than a tough time in boxing training, and I'm at fault for not being more aware. I apologize."

Teal blushed and shifted on her back paws. She grimaced at the fresh blisters that had grown on top of existing ones. Warp speed skipping, long after everyone else received Rocket Ron's nod to stop, meant Teal's sensitive feet never got the chance to heal.

Teal thought she might treat herself and dip those blistered paws in the Unfathomable Lake on the way ho—on the way to wherever she would go. Her head lowered into her shoulders.

"Teal, are you listening?" Darcy said.

Teal jumped. "Yes, ma´am."

"Because of your harsh treatment in boxing, we agree that you should at least be allowed to complete your last day. Go to Freddie's class."

Teal wanted to run up to Darcy, grab her face with both paws, and kiss her snout. Instead, she nodded and padded out of the room.

Freddie's class now only consisted of the finalists: three cats, two ferrets, and a human. Oh, and of course a rabbit, although, she couldn't count herself since she'd already had her exit interview.

Freddie swaggered up and down the orange stage, shoulders swaying, firing his review questions at them.

"Why do we want to be Switchers?" he asked.

"To help the beings on Earth!" they replied in unison.

"The three don'ts on Earth for animals?" He raised his shades with a paw.

"No smiling, talking, or other advanced behaviour in front of humans."

"Number one rule as a Switcher?"

"Respect, Respect, Respect."

"What's the Switcher chant?"

"HAR! HAR! HAR!" they screamed, jumping up on their seats, raising fists in the air.

"Tell me what it means," Freddie said.

"Honesty, Awareness, Re-spon-si-bi-li-ty."

"Deaf as a post with these things, man." Freddie grinned and cupped a paw to his ear.

"HONESTY, AWARENESS, RE-SPON-SI-BI-LI-TY." They screamed so loud, twenty-three empty seats rattled.

"Yeah, man." Freddie nodded at them all, his mouth raised on one side. Someone knocked on the door.

Zeus walked in. "We're voting."

"Way to go, all of you," Freddie said. "Go get some chow. I'll see you back here for the final exam and the announcement." He jumped off the stage and followed Zeus.

Freddie stood back on the podium, the only noise a few stomach rumbles. Not many recruits could eat on voting day. Teal, being a rabbit, had a stomach that never shut up even though she always ate.

Darcy, Zeus, and Rocket Ron Johnson stood at the back of the room.

"We've done the merits," Freddie said. "It's a close run thing. Everything hangs on this last exam."

Zeus walked up to Teal, his voice-activated cart following him.

"Stop," he said. He took the top test pod out of the cart, placed it in front of her, and went on to the next recruit.

Teal looked down at the silver machine—her name written in gold across the centre. She ran her paw over the embossed letters.

"Open 'em up," Freddie said.

Teal tapped on her name. The test pod opened and the screen lit up green.

With no keyboard, just two round pads—red for yes, blue for no—they hit a pad in answer to the questions that appeared on screen.

"Darcy's got the mother pod," Freddie said. "Your results will download to her as usual."

Teal looked over her shoulder and saw the golden machine open in front of Darcy.

"Today's exam's different," Freddie said. "Six hundred questions and only six seconds to read and answer each question."

The other recruits all looked at each other, eyes wide.

Teal smiled. She loved time pressure exams. Sure, she knew it didn't matter how well she did, she'd lost her chance, but she could still have fun. Her paws hovered over the pads.

"Go for it," Freddie said.

The first question appeared on the screen: *Switchers are an elaborate group—human or animal—that trade places with Earthies.*

Easy! Teal hit the red button.

The next question appeared: *Switchers go to Earth for six weeks and must complete three missions—one every two weeks.*

Yes, yes, yes! Teal hit the red button and grinned.

Dyads, also known as Pure Mayas or Super Switchers, have the ability to transform into any Earthie—human or animal.

Red again!

The Earthies you swap places with come to Joya to learn nothing—just to have fun.

They wish! Teal hit the blue pad.

The questions kept flying and Teal kept batting the answers back. She had never read so fast in her life. Tap on the red pad, three on the blue, back to the red. Her adrenalin never stopped pumping.

The screen went red to signal the end of the test. Teal rested back on her haunches. The other recruits exhaled like a collective gust of wind.

Freddie jumped off the stage and went to confer with Darcy.

Zeus came around and packed the test pods into his cart. Teal grinned.

A week ago she'd been flying around in that cart in the Super Ramp Room—the best prize so far for winning the weekly exam.

Zeus shouted to the cart: "Spin!" "Super fast!" "Backwards!" "Up on two wheels!" Teal squealed and hung on for dear life, amid the cheers from the other recruits.

Freddie returned to the stage and cleared his throat. Everyone shifted in their seats.

Teal knew Candy would get it. An intelligent white fluffy cat, and she came from a Switcher family. All trainees had studied their Blibs, which delivered footage of animals and people on Earth. But no one studied more than Candy. She already had plans for how to help an unloved dog and an undernourished ferret.

"No point dragging this out, man," Freddie said. "You're all hot to get this far, but only one gets to be a Switcher and part of our team. Our original decision stands."

The trainees looked across at each other. Teal could see them twitching. She'd have been chewing her own cheeks if she were still in the running.

"White, fluffy, and full of personality," Freddie said.

Teal nodded at the similarity between her and Candy. They looked at each other and grinned.

"The Switcher is ..." Freddie looked at them all. "Teal!"

Teal shot a glance at Candy, whose teeth looked sharp all of a sudden. She looked up at Freddie, her eyes pleading for an explanation.

Freddie burst out laughing.

Very funny, and sick. Didn't he know how awful she felt already? Her lips trembling, she jumped off her chair and rushed to the back of the room before tears could spill. Darcy, Zeus, and Rocket Ron all stood in front of the door.

Zeus smiled down at her.

"Well done, Teal, great to have you on board."

"Huh?" Teal said.

"Teal, you're the first rabbit Switcher," Darcy said. "Congratulations."

"But you said, the respect thing . . ."

"Quite right," Darcy said. "And you'll do well to learn your lesson, but you've passed every exam with more stars than any other trainee, your boxing assessment surpassed some established Switchers, and you saved yourself in the exit interview."

"But—"

"You embodied the Switcher motto. Honest with Freddie, Aware, and Responsible for your actions listed by Zeus. You didn't waste our time with excuses. HAR, HAR, HAR, indeed!"

"Took it on the chin," Rocket Ron said, and tapped his own chin with his fist.

"Is this a joke?" Teal asked. "Why did Freddie laugh?" She looked around to see Candy crying in Freddie's arms.

Darcy smiled down at Teal.

"You have no idea of your talent, that's why. I want you on my team. You're clever, intuitive, and always ahead of the game."

Teal felt her open mouth stretch into a smile as big as her face. Her stomach did somersaults.

"I'll take you to Earth myself tonight," Darcy said. "First I need to break the news to Hi Brid."

Teal wanted to flip herself around and fly up and down the room.

Darcy pushed the door to leave, then turned to Teal.

"Might be an idea to make up with your father before you leave."

Chapter 2

Down on Earth, by the outskirts of London, England, Julius Webb sat in the black swivel chair in his laboratory at the back of the house.

How had it happened? He ran a hand through his wild hair. In the ten years he'd been working with the secret services on both sides of the Atlantic, he'd never been careless. Never.

He closed his laptop and stared at the jam jar of lime-green truth serum.

He had followed the CIA's exact specifications—so why did the truth serum now contain a deadly virus? He'd put it in there somehow. Worse, he couldn't extract it.

He threw his half-eaten sandwich in the bin beside him and took a sip of his peppermint tea. Did he know anyone with the skill to extract it?

An image popped into his brain: A beautiful woman with long brown hair and brown eyes, wearing a red dress. Julius had his arms around her. They stood in some exotic place, laughing. It didn't make any sense. He wouldn't have forgotten a woman *that* stunning.

He needed a rest. His friend the queen had told Julius not to take on this latest CIA project.

He felt something hot in his lap and looked down. He'd spilled his peppermint tea. He got up and went to the bathroom.

Julius looked in the bathroom mirror, unhappy with the reflection. A man of forty, exclamation-mark hair, smudged glasses, sickly yellow skin, and a peppermint tea stain down the front of his white coat that looked like he'd wet himself. Julius still had strength from his rugby days, but the mirror didn't show it.

The memory of the beautiful woman flashed before his eyes again. Julius smiled. The memory smiled back and winked at him. Julius rushed back to his lab, and searched for vacation spots on his laptop. The CIA could wait.

The internet listed thousands of holidays in the UK. Or did he want to go abroad?

He saw an ad: *Fly to the moon! Five-day holiday in luxury rocket. Check available dates.*

This sounded more like it. Julius clicked the search key.

Something seemed familiar about the photo of the rocket. Julius took off his glasses, leaned back in his chair, and massaged the bridge of his nose.

Another image flashed in front of him: The woman and Julius flying through the air on a rocket, riding it like a broom. Ridiculous.

He needed some fresh air. He locked the jam jar away in his safe and left the lab. He'd call Agent Shatner later, tell him about the serum. He snatched his keys and walked to the front of the house.

Julius walked through his neighbourhood and beyond, oblivious to his surroundings. He stuck his hands in his lab coat and felt his penknife in his left coat pocket. He ran his fingers over the cold metal handle. Where had he gone wrong with the serum?

He became aware of some people in front of him and stepped to the side. They didn't move. He looked up and took a deep breath.

Three young men stood in front of him. They didn't look as if they wanted to make conversation. All unshaven, the one in the middle looked Hispanic and wore a white T-shirt. The other two had shaved heads and pasty skin. They could do with a bit of their friend's colour. Julius grinned.

"What's so funny?" the scrawny skinhead asked.

Julius tightened his grip on the knife.

"You deaf or somethin?"

Julius looked around to get his bearings. He saw a woman across the road run into her house.

"Hey, I'm talking to you."

"Look, I don't want any trouble."

"Should've thought about that before you decided to be so ignorant. Looks like we've scared 'im."

Julius looked down at his lab coat—the stain. A fist flew from the right. Julius blocked it with his right arm and threw a left hook. The scrawny pasty-face went down as if all the bones in his legs had shattered.

Julius flipped open his knife and watched the other two's eyes widen.

"What, lads? Not armed?"

The other pasty-face raised a fist. Julius ducked, punched him in the stomach, and watched him double over.

The Hispanic lunged forward. Julius stepped back, threw a weak left, and shot his head to the left. The Hispanic's fist flew past his ear.

Julius retracted his left arm and saw blood on the knife.

The Hispanic looked at his arm and the blood seeping through his T-shirt. His mouth fell open. He clutched his arm and ran off.

Julius heard a groan and looked down. The scrawny pasty-face seemed in no rush to leave the ground. The other just gaped at him.

Where did I learn to fight like that? A memory came and went before he could grab it.

Julius heard the police sirens. He looked down at the red blood on his knife, on his hand. Red like a … like a red and purple planet. An earthquake of memories erupted in his mind.

Teal jumped into the Unfathomable Lake. She surfaced from the vivid green water and floated on her back. A Switcher! She propelled herself in circles and shouted with delight.

She got out of the water, stretched out on the soft purple sponge field, and smiled up at the sky. She thought of the earthie rabbits on the Blib transmissions. She would soon be one of them.

Sure, she'd have to eat a lot of that hay stuff down there instead of real food, and restrict her actions big time so she looked and acted like an earthie, but in a few hours she would be flying to Earth. And Darcy would be taking her! Darcy, who had kept her paws planted on Joya for years.

Wild stories flew around training as to why the best Switcher in history had stopped switching. Teal knew why. She had checked the log book in the main hall, had done the calculations.

Darcy's last return in the log to Joya had been on Teal's first birthday—the day her mum died.

The two arresting officers, PC Frank Willis and PC Alan Black, stood outside the Chief Inspector's office.

"Get in here now!" Chief Inspector Burns said.

"That man you've nicked is Julius Webb. He's a famous scientist, we can't keep him in a cell. He's friends with the prime minister, the chancellor ..." He shook his head.

"With all due *respect*," Frank said, "he had a weapon in his hand, covered in blood."

"That's not the point, and it's only a penknife."

"What are you saying?" Alan asked. "Someone kills someone, we check if they're friends with the prime minister, and if they are, we say, 'That's okay, mate, you run along?'"

"Release Julius Webb now!" Burns looked as if all the veins in his forehead would burst.

The two officers muttered but left to release the great scientist. When they got to the cell, Julius Webb refused to leave.

After two hours, Frank sent his partner home. No point in him and Alan both staying. Frank introduced himself, but the scientist just stared into space, then burst into tears.

Teal twitched her nose as she approached the cave—white vinegar wafted through the open window. Her dad always scrubbed everything when something upset him.

She got up on her hind legs and looked through the open window. He tore around the cave, vinegar bottle in one hand, duster in the other. She knew his keen nose had sensed her.

"Dad, I've got some amazing news."

He grunted. She had to speak to his back.

"I've done it, Dad. They chose me. Your daughter is the first ever rabbit Switcher!"

The vinegar bottle crashed to the floor. He turned to face her, tears in his eyes. Teal gulped.

"I just want you to be proud."

"*Proud?*" He shook his head. "I'm going to lose you, too."

"But I've been trained. I. . ."

He stormed over, shut the window in her face and pulled the curtains.

Teal swallowed the rock wedged in her throat and looked down at her feet. The crystals in the Unfathomable Lake had soothed her blisters. Shame they couldn't work their magic on heartache.

Her instinct told her to look up. A black beast with a white head and huge wings plummeted towards her. She flung herself to the ground, as flat as she could, and closed her eyes.

"That's your idea of protecting yourself, is it?" the beast said.

Teal opened an eye. The wings enveloped her. A claw grabbed her by the neck and lifted her skyward.

She flew backwards across the sky at twice the speed of Freddie's Harley. She noticed the Unfathomable Lake beneath her, and that's when the beast released its grip.

Teal screamed. She fell through the air, pointed her paws at the last minute, and plunged beneath the water. The lake swallowed her. She thrashed against the water with her hind legs and thrust herself up with her forepaws.

Her head emerged from the lake. She saw the black beast swoop towards her. She tried to swim to the edge, but her legs felt heavy. The eels!

They dragged her under. She swallowed mouthfuls of the salty lake. She kicked against them but they tightened their hold.

Her lungs, frantic for air, pushed against her ribcage. The eels coiled their bodies around her limbs, one curled around her chest. She looked up at the surface of the water.

A giant shadow descended above her until it blocked out the light. The beast broke through the surface and lunged beneath the water. Teal shut her eyes. She felt the beast's talons grip her head, and it yanked her skyward. She launched out of the water and up into the air. She coughed, and water flew out of her nose and mouth.

The eels released their grip. Teal heard them splash back into the lake. The beast relaxed its grip around her skull, and the pain in her head eased.

The talons opened above the great red oak on the edge of the lake, and she landed with a thud. She rubbed her head, then checked her paws for blood.

The black beast perched beside her in the tree. Teal steadied herself in a bed of twigs and mud.

"A nest." She looked from the beast to the bed. "You're ... you're an *eagle*."

The eagle nodded and tucked its black wings around him like a cloak.

"But you can't be. There are no eagles on Joya."

Teal gulped. All Mayas worshipped the eagle, but like a God, not in the flesh and feather. She'd studied them in other cultures. They ate animals much bigger than her. If she jumped he'd catch her in a second.

"I'm not of this plane," the eagle said. "I'm your Spirit Guide."

"What? So, you're not going to eat me?"

"Not today, no."

Teal let out a breath, then gaped at the eagle. "My Spirit Guide? Eagles are like the most revered spirits on the planet."

The eagle nodded.

"How come *I* got an eagle?"

"I wonder myself sometimes," the eagle said.

"How come I've never seen you before? I meditate every day."

"You haven't needed to see me before now."

Teal slumped in the nest.

"Why do you think I dropped you in the lake?" the eagle said.

"Because I'm too heavy?" Teal put her paws over her tummy. "I've been meaning to cut down."

The eagle spread his wings and stuck out his breast. "I could lift ten of you."

Teal didn't doubt it.

"Uh, I don't know, then."

"To show you the perils of pity. Have the eels ever attacked before?"

Teal shook her head. "They never attack, only when … so you dropped me knowing they'd drown me? You knew that they attack weakness."

"Who pulled you out? Would you have understood a more subtle message?"

Teal chose not to answer.

"Negative emotions are for weak minds."

"But I just want my dad to. . ."

"To what? Dance around the cave because you could get yourself killed?"

Teal went to argue, but the eagle raised a talon.

"I tell you this. You will go to Earth. You will not be deterred. Do not expect one who smells death to understand."

Teal gulped. "Do *you* think I should go?"

The eagle shrugged. "I will not waste words on closed ears, but know this—you go alone. Maya Spirit Guides cannot leave Joya."

Julius Webb sat in the police cell amid handfuls of sodden tissues. Forgotten scenes ripped through his heart. His mind, a forest of retrieved memories, burst at his skull. He'd read once about a suicide note a man had left that said his brain was too full. Julius now understood the pain of it.

Six years of lost memories back with him after *sixteen* years. Too much at once. He needed some space. The pain in his head banged in his ears, and he felt sick.

Arabella—the love of his life—had slipped Missing Memory potion in his tea! He shook his head. Darcy, her *hallowed* boss, would have forced her.

"I loved her. How could she?"

"So it's a woman, then?"

Julius looked at the wiry policeman. His black hair cut close to his head made his green eyes stand out.

"Frank Willis." The officer held out his hand again.

Julius shook it.

"Broke your heart, did she?"

Julius nodded and dug his fist into his chest. Arabella did extra switches and snuck him onto Joya, putting him in the luggage part of the rocket when they arrived by day. Not an easy trip scrunched up in a ball. Not an easy relationship. But it had been worth it.

Why couldn't Darcy keep her snout out? She had taken *everything*.

"Hurt her back," Frank said.

Julius rubbed his eyes with a fist. He looked at Frank.

Yes. He would make *Darcy* hurt.

Frank's eyes lit up when Julius invited him in for coffee.

Julius didn't mention that Arabella came from another planet and flew around on a rocket. He wanted Frank to feel sorry for him, not question his sanity.

He told him she had snuck something in his drink. He didn't say it was Missing Memory potion, an infusion that until now had repressed his memories of Arabella and anything connected with Joya.

"She tried to poison you? We can arrest her for attempted murder. You're a famous scientist, poison her back. Uh, forget I said that."

Julius looked at the policeman and smiled. He could use the deadly truth serum.

Chapter 3

Teal picked at a twig with her forepaw.

"Couldn't you just pop down—check I'm okay?" she said.

The eagle looked around the great red oak and shook his head.

"Are you allergic to listening?" he said. "I told you Spirit Guides can't leave Joya."

"But what if I'm in danger?"

"You're going to Earth, not the Open Circus. Of course you'll be in danger."

Teal started scratching behind her ear with her hind leg. She couldn't stop.

"Enough," the eagle said. "Look. The best I can do is send you messages in your dreams. You do know how to read your dreams?"

Teal shook her head. The eagle closed his eyes.

"We better have a practice. Before you go to sleep, you decide to remember your dreams, okay?"

Teal nodded.

"When you wake up, rerun the dreams instantly—before you lose them. See if you can figure out what the messages are. Ready?"

"I think so."

The eagle wrapped its wings over Teal's head, and her body slumped into the nest.

She woke up on the front step of the Switcher Centre, to the noise of Darcy's YZ400F landing in front of her. She rubbed her eyes and gazed at the blue bike. She looked around—her Spirit Guide had gone. Dreams! Okay, think. Um, Freddie telling her Earth didn't need another Switcher. What did that mean?

Darcy lifted the goggles from her eyes. "Have you seen your dad, Teal?"

"Huh? Oh, no. Well, yes, but only through the window, he's angry."

Darcy bit her lip. "You can turn down being a Switcher. I can drop you home, make him take you back in."

Teal shook her head. Guilt slithered in her tummy. Her dad would throw a fit if Darcy turned up at the cave.

"Fair enough," Darcy said. She threw Teal a helmet. "On you get."

Teal put on the helmet and ran up the best bike on the planet. The bike hummed through her paws.

"All set?" Darcy sped off before Teal could answer.

They raced up a steep hill and Darcy pulled up at the top.

"Here it is, the exit to Earth track."

Teal looked to her right at the giant golden slide they would speed down and fly off into space. It looked pretty steep.

"Four hundred metres," Darcy said.

Teal gulped.

Darcy said some coordinates. A translucent shield edged in gold appeared before them and lowered into the ground.

Darcy drove around and lined the bike up.

"Here we go."

She pulled back her paw and revved the throttle. The growl of the bike thundered through Teal's body. She clung to Darcy's back. The bike shot forward and they flew down the steep golden slide. Teal's stomach vaulted. As they dropped off the edge of the planet, the blackness swallowed Teal's scream.

They dropped through the sky, and the fear in her stomach spread through her veins to the tips of her paws. She screwed up her eyes and waited for the crash.

And then they slowed. She opened her eyes and her mouth fell open. They floated down inside a transparent funnel, encased in a golden corkscrew.

She felt light-headed as they touched down on Earth. She slid off the bike, and her nostrils filled with a beautiful smell like clean fresh green vegetables.

"Mmm," she said. "What's that smell?"

"Grass. Earth's equivalent to our purple sponge fields, minus the bounce."

Darcy jumped off the bike and handed Teal two darts.

"Go into that garden and inject the two rabbits as quick as you can. Bring me the white one, the one you're switching with. Her name's Jen."

"Uh, aren't you going to introduce me or something?" Teal said.

"Me? Kill them?"

"What?" Teal looked at the darts in her paw.

"Earth rabbits can die from shock. Dogs are predators here."

Teal gulped.

"Remember," Darcy said, "throw fast and light, like a jab."

Teal nodded and ran off.

The shed door had two halves, a latch over both. She took a deep breath. She jumped up, lifted the lower latch with her nose, and burst into the shed.

She looked left. A rabbit covered in black and white splodges sat on the ground floor of a five-storey wire cage. Teal threw the tranquilizer, and the rabbit slumped.

She scanned the cage for the other rabbit. Nothing. She heard a crunch to her right. The white rabbit stood in the corner of the shed. It looked from Teal to the unconscious rabbit in the cage. It dropped the hay from its mouth and started to shake. Teal threw the dart.

She ran over and sank her teeth into the scruff of the rabbit's neck. Then she hauled the rabbit backwards across the shed and out into the garden, grateful now to Rocket Ron for the intense training.

She reached Darcy, spat out some fur, and massaged her jaw. Darcy beamed. She took the floppy rabbit and placed her on the back of the bike.

Teal frowned. "I didn't get her quick enough. She started to shake."

Darcy put a paw over the rabbit's heart. "Earthie animals—unlike humans—have no fear of us on Joya. She'll be fine."

Teal nodded.

Darcy raised her arm. "It's time. Paw."

Teal placed her paw under Darcy's, the way she'd been shown, and closed her eyes. She felt Darcy's paw pass straight through hers, and her insides became weightless. She struggled to keep her feet on the floor. She looked up expecting to see her own paw on top, but Darcy's great black paw hadn't moved.

Darcy looked at her and smiled.

"Go back inside. Your body will switch into Jen's in a few minutes."

Teal looked at the rabbit draped on the bike, her hind feet as big as her body. She looked down at her own neat little ones.

"Know what you mean," Darcy said. "Biggest feet I ever saw. You'll get used to them. Any questions?"

Teal shook her head.

"Okay. Here's your Magi Pod. We'll download your assignment tonight. I'm giving you two days instead of one to settle in. You've seen earth rabbit footage, you know how to act."

Darcy revved the engine and flew off into the sky.

Teal heard a rustle and looked right. A red dog with a pointy nose and a bushy tail narrowed his eyes and licked his lips. Teal bolted to the shed and got herself inside just in time.

Her whole body tingled, and her feet hurt. She looked down—and saw her toes shoot out in front of her. Her fur rose and fell, as if a million fur mites jumped up and down under her skin. She wanted to scratch the imaginary creatures away. Her body sagged. It felt heavy—it *was* heavy.

She looked up at the black and white rabbit as if to say, *did you see that?* But he didn't look as though he'd seen much at all.

Teal ran a pad over her softer fur, looked down at her new feet, and grinned. She walked three steps into the giant cage and landed on her nose. She burst out laughing, rolling on the warm mat at the bottom of the cage, a cage big enough for twenty rabbits. This could be fun.

Julius Webb woke after a night of dreams mingled with new memories. He felt wet fabric against his cheek. He threw the pillow across the room, sat on the edge of the bed, and pushed his palm into his forehead.

The pain had been with him since the memories returned. He'd eaten his way through half a bottle of painkillers, but nothing touched it. Darcy had a lot to answer for.

He went to the kitchen, made a peppermint tea, and took it through to the living room. He sank into one of the dark brown leather sofas.

He had to get Darcy down on Earth. He thought for a minute. Arabella used to marvel at how the great Darcy could scan the newspapers from twelve countries every day before breakfast.

He reached for the phone and made an international call to his contact, Agent Shatner, at the CIA.

"Julius?" Shatner said. "Do you know what time it is here?"

"I'm exhausted. I'm retiring."

"And our truth serum?"

"Haven't done it."

"Hey, I don't want to have to threaten you with breach of contract, buddy."

"Then don't. I'm retired." Julius hung up and pulled the phone cord out of the wall. He sprang to his feet and kicked the black beanbag.

Darcy Maya would pay.

He grabbed his keys and headed for the police station to see his new friend.

Teal woke to see a blond thin teenager placing a cardboard tunnel inside the cage, his legs so long that as he squatted in front of her, his knees reached his ears. She recognized Jon from the Blib transmissions. His turquoise sweater matched those big, gentle eyes; his thin mouth drooped down and conveyed the sadness within. The sooner he got to Joya, the better.

Teal went to smile at him, then stopped herself.

"Hello, Jen," Jon said. "You're up late. What's up with Max?"

Teal heard paws running above her and looked up.

"Look, I'm late for school," Jon said. "I'll try and get home lunchtime to let you out for a bit." He stroked the top of Teal's head, frowned at Max, and left.

Teal ran up to the second floor. Max rubbed his chin all over the cage like a duster. He jumped when he saw Teal.

"I must have needed that sleep," Teal said. "Should've been up before you." She rubbed her eyes.

Max flew up the next flight and scraped his chin over every bit of the cage.

"Hey!" Teal shouted. "You can wear your chin down to the bone or you can let me explain. Your choice."

Max stopped. He looked down at her. "How come you can speak?"

"News flash. In case you didn't notice, so can you."

"What?!"

"Not to everyone and only while I'm here," Teal said. "Any chance you can come down a level and we can talk?"

Max rubbed his chin on a bit more cage, hopped down, and went to the furthest corner.

"What's with the chin thing?" Teal asked.

"Mark my territory. I know you're not Jen. You smell different."

Teal lifted an arm and had a sniff. "Hmm, you could be right."

"What have you done with Jen?"

"We've switched places. She's on my planet for six weeks and I'm here."

"Planet?" Max began to shake.

PC Frank Willis jutted out his chin and looked around at his colleagues. Julius laughed to himself. The officer left the station with his new friend, a swagger in his step.

Julius watched Frank slide into the Porsche and breathe in the leather.

"What a car!"

"You can drive it back if you like."

"Are you *serious*?"

Julius nodded and grinned.

"Frank, you really helped me yesterday. I'm taking your valuable advice. I'm going to hurt her back."

Frank wore the flattery like a breastplate.

"I'm going to give the story to the press about the fight, say I don't feel well and am retiring."

"How will that—"

"It won't, but what you say will."

Once Max calmed down, Teal ate some hay. She'd been putting it off, but her stomach growled like a dog. She stuffed it down and it came back up.

"Wow. That's impressive," Max said.

"Being sick, or being brave enough to eat this dry stuff with no sauce?" Teal's stomach yearned for lasagne and chocolate fudge brownies.

"The vomit thing. Earth rabbits can't."

"You're kidding?"

"Nope. Only comes out one end."

"Wow." Teal grabbed some raspberry leaves, turned her nose up, and opened her mouth. Not exactly raspberry jam but better than hay.

"So what's this Jon like, then?" Teal said, and gulped down some more leaves.

"He's great. We normally get out twice a day. He ordered this rabbit condo on the internet for us." Max looked around the cage. "We've got five floors, loads of tunnels, hay, toys to chew, plus the run of the shed."

"Don't Earth rabbits prefer to live inside?"

"Jon sneaks Jen in sometimes, but I prefer the cold. Do you live inside on your planet?"

"Yeah, we've all got our own house."

"Blimey."

"Well, ours is actually a cave, two bedrooms. It's not the best area on Joya, but Dad … keeps the cave spotless." Teal looked down at her paws.

"You okay?" Max asked.

"Yeah, sure, I just wish you'd let me open the shed door so I could get out for a while."

"No. This is a dangerous place for rabbits."

Where had she heard that before?

"I can look after myself," she said.

"I don't care. If Jon's mum comes home and we're out …" Max shook his head. "He gets enough grief at school."

"Why?" Teal asked.

"A boy, Pigbreath, bullies him. He offloads on us when he gets home."

"Does his mum know?"

"No idea. She's not happy herself."

"What's wrong with—?"

"His dad left a year ago. Jon blames himself. His mum told him it had nothing to do with him, but Jon gave up football, thought his dad might come back."

"What?"

"His dad coached the team. Jon missed a penalty. If he hadn't, they'd have won the trophy. I heard his dad screaming at him before they pulled up. His dad left the next day. Pigbreath and the others kept telling him his dad left because he was ashamed of his son. Pigbreath's bullied him ever since."

Poor Jon, no wonder they wanted him up on Joya.

"Hey, will we be able to talk to Jon?" Max said.

"He won't be able to hear *you*, and I'm not allowed to talk to humans."

"Oh." Max's long ears drooped.

"Don't worry. He won't be around for long."

"What?" Max's fur stood up, and he growled.

She really did need to think before she spoke.

Chapter 4

Teal couldn't remember the download code for the assignment. She'd tried three times. The Magi Pod would crash if she got it wrong again.

She heard Jon come through the gate and stuffed the Magi Pod under some hay in the corner of the shed.

Jon let them out into the garden, and Teal headed straight for the grass. Hay might be inedible, but grass set off sprinklers of saliva in her mouth.

Jon made tunnels. Max and Teal ran through them and all over Jon. They listened as he told them about Pigbreath's bullying. Not being able to help made Teal want to tear her fur out. It took a nip on the ear from Max to stop her from speaking.

She wished Jon didn't have to go to school. She snuggled into him at every opportunity, hoping her happiness would rub off. His kindness had rubbed off on her. She was so engrossed in the diversions of Earth and her new friend's problems that her assignment slipped her mind.

Darcy stretched on her bed and yawned. The Earth papers shot out of her revolving library and hit her in the snout. She huffed, settled down to scan them, and choked on her dental stick. Her eyes raced from one headline to another. She bit her lip until it bled.

"You're right to worry."

Darcy looked up at In′Lakesh, her Spirit Guide. The aura around the unicorn glowed a white more intense than her body, and a violet beam emitted from her spiral horn.

Darcy snatched the papers in her mouth and ran to the Assembly Room. Hi Brid, First Seat on the Maya Council, ate breakfast there. He preferred it to the noise of the kitchen.

Darcy barked at the doors. They opened and she rushed in.

"So much for a quiet breakfast." Hi Brid tightened his thin lips and lowered his eyelids over his brown-black eyes.

Malcolm, Third Seat on the Council and best gymnast on the planet, sat next to Hi Brid. Malcolm's bald head gave a clue to his age, but his body could have belonged to a twenty-year-old. He raised a bacon sandwich to his lips, his biceps bulging.

Darcy dropped the papers from her mouth. "Something's wrong."

"We gathered. Care to enlighten us before our breakfast goes cold?" Hi Brid pulled his sleek black hair into a ponytail and placed it over his muscular chest.

"Julius Webb is in all the national newspapers on Earth."

Malcolm dropped his bacon sandwich. The name hadn't been mentioned for a long time.

"He's retired." Darcy said.

"And?" Hi Brid said.

"He was in a fight—"

"That's *it*?"

Malcolm picked up his sandwich and put it back together.

"It does seem like you have your snout in a twist over nothing. He has the right to retire, like everyone else."

She picked up a newspaper and read a couple of sentences aloud:

> PC Frank Willis took the scientist to the hospital because of a slight concussion. He said, 'I got worried when the scientist started talking about flying on a *rocket.*'

Malcolm picked a bit of bacon off his bread. "You think he's remembered?"

"Oh, for goodness sake," Hi Brid said. "It doesn't mean anything."

"We should investigate," Darcy said.

"Oh, I see. An investigation which needs approval from the Top *Four* Seats of the Maya Council?"

Darcy closed her eyes. She'd always known this problem would come back to haunt her.

"In'Lakesh said—"

"You should be concentrating on that rabbit," Hi Brid said. "Four days—and nothing. What's Teal doing? Get down there. You know what to do."

Darcy stormed from the room and crashed into Cool T in the entrance hall. She wiggled her snout, shook her head, and looked up at the mountain of a man. Eleventh Seat on the Council only because he refused a higher place every time she offered.

"You okay?" he said. She looked over her shoulder.

"I need you to do something for me. I want you to go to Earth and visit Julius Webb. You'll be the Chancellor. They're friends."

"I'm switching with an *adult*?" Cool T said.

"You're not switching with him, so make sure you're not seen. We can't afford to have two sightings."

"*What?*"

"You've only got an hour. We can't afford an imbalance."

"But that's against the—"

"Yes, it is."

Teal's frustration built up like a giant fur ball. She wanted to bite Pigbreath. Why couldn't he leave Jon alone? Why didn't Jon fight back? Not being able to help made her irritable. She imagined her teeth piercing Pigbreath's skin.

"You bit me!" Jon said. He threw Teal into the shed and sucked his finger, then stormed off. Teal heard the back door slam.

Max shook his head at her. She hadn't *meant* to do it.

"Hh hum!"

Teal spun around to see Darcy throw a dart at Max.

"Oh, no."

"Oh, yes," Darcy said.

"But ... I didn't hear your bike."

Darcy closed the shed door. "Having a good time, are you?"

"Oh my gosh, I'm on the wrong planet. It's amazing down here. The grass is so moreish, no wonder the cows love it. There are these great things called frogs that hop all the time, they're just like rabbits, well, not *exactly*, they don't have fur and big ears or a tail, and the handshake's a bit slimy. Do you know they jump so they don't leave a scent behind? Did I mention the grass? The name Jen suits me, don't you think? In fact, don't call me Teal, call me Jen."

Teal paused to breathe.

"Have you even downloaded your assignment, *Teal*?"

Teal's whiskers drooped.

"Max sort of ate the download code."

"What!?" Darcy said. A growl came from deep within her stomach.

Teal's eyes shot over to Max, who lay on his side, tongue hanging out.

"Well, you know how forgetful I can be when I get excited, so I wrote the code on a piece of lettuce, and. . . well. . ."

"Listen, Teal. Hi Brid wants me to bring you back and put someone more experienced in the role."

"I can do it, Darcy. Honest I can."

"How can we trust you? You haven't even checked in with the daily learnings."

"I will, I will, got a bit carried away with the grass, and meeting the local frogs and stuff, I'm focused now, really I am."

"You know the deadlines—three assignments in six weeks, two weeks for each assignment. Do you think you can complete the first one now, in ten days?"

Teal hung her head and looked down at her super-sized feet.

Darcy sighed, turned off the visual badge on her shoulder, and lowered her voice.

"The code will appear within the next sixty seconds. You have one hour to process the assignment and put forward a proposal. If all members of the Council accept your proposal, you can stay. I can do no more. We have to take the boy tonight. We're way behind schedule."

Of course. *They* would help Jon. Teal jumped forward and licked Darcy's paws.

Darcy jolted her head back and pulled her paws away. "What are you *doing?*"

"If an Earth bunny licks your face or your hands, she's happy."

Darcy shook her head. "Whatever." She opened the shed door and headed down the garden.

"I won't let you down, Darcy," Teal said.

"You'd better not," Darcy said. "And stop smiling."

Cool T parked his quad bike behind Julius Webb's shed, out of sight of the back of the house. He ran his hands through his mop of black hair. Fancy *Darcy* breaking the law. He smiled and shook his head.

He looked down the garden. The double gates at the bottom opened onto a park. The garden, the size of half a football field, had shoulder-high cacti along the borders. The shed with padlocked double doors stood a few metres from the house and looked more like a log cabin. Hell, Julius could rent it out to a family.

Cool T shifted in his seat and glanced around the garden. All clear. He focused his mind on the chancellor and tilted his head back. Fat erupted beneath his skin, and his body inflated. His fingers became like sausages on the handlebars. He felt a mallet bash the top of his skull, and his height diminished.

Layers of fat engulfed the bike. Cool T heaved himself up, pulled at his right leg, and ended up on his back in the grass. His breath sounded like someone snoring. He rolled onto his front, hoisted himself up, and wiped the sweat from his forehead.

He reached over and pressed the cerise button on the handlebar. The Shadow Veil descended over the bike. Cool T could still see the outline of the quad, but to all Earthies it would be invisible. He waddled over to Julius's back door.

The sweet fruity scent of the thousand strawberry-leaved oak trees filled Darcy's nostrils. She looked down on the sea of red leaves, tightened her grip around the handlebars, and lowered her bike. She manoeuvred between the trees and touched down on the black stone path. The trees rustled a welcome as she rode up to the Maya Castle.

The immense purple building resembled a giant horseshoe. It had four turrets. A lime-green sculpted swirly top adorned each turret, the same lime-green as the arched front door.

Darcy jumped off her bike, placed a paw on the door, and waited for the scan. The lime-green door glided to the side. She headed for the Assembly Room and took a deep breath outside the red double doors. The most traditional on the Council, Hi Brid had the patience of a peanut.

She had made the most of the loop trick on her bike on the way back, and now she needed to give Teal as much time as possible. Darcy closed her eyes. That rabbit had talent, just like her mother.

She barked and the doors opened. The yellow sponge floor had a covering of red, orange, and green cushions all bigger than Darcy. The bare lilac brick walls had an assortment of blinds at the ceiling that dropped to give decoration for parties. The ceiling, a cluster of Maya dust, glistened silver.

Danny Loco, Fourth Seat on the Council, noticed her first. He was only sixteen and already a professor. Joya had never had a better scientist.

"Yo, Darcy. What's up? Think Teal's got a crack at it?" Danny Loco stuck a hand in his white coat and flattened his wild hair with the other.

"Yes, I do. Do you?"

"Not sure. She's so hyper. A straitjacket might help." He flopped down on a fuchsia cushion.

Freddie and Zeus, both stretched out on green cushions, burst out laughing.

Darcy looked over at Hi Brid. He had his face buried in his hands. He shook his head. His shiny black hair swam about his shoulders like eels from the lake.

"Sorry," Darcy said.

Hi Brid looked up. His brown-black eyes narrowed like arrows.

"Sorry? Since when does a Council Member turn off their visual receiver? You've given her another chance, haven't you?"

Darcy looked over at the big Magi screen and ran a paw over her badge. She'd never been wrong about a Switcher before.

"I've given her an hour. Let's just see what she comes up with."

Julius finished his call. Graham Drum had no time for anyone but himself. Julius didn't like his tax plans one bit, friend or not. There had never been a more corrupt chancellor.

He heard a knock at the back door, got up from his black chair, and looked out the lab window into the garden. It couldn't be.

He opened the door.

"How can you be … I've just …" Julius pointed in the direction of his lab. His mobile sat on his desk.

"Uh, I came through the park to avoid the paparazzi."

Julius saw a flashing purple light in the pocket of the chancellor's trousers. His stomach leapt, and he fought to keep his face neutral.

"Your mobile's flashing."

The chancellor looked down and frowned. "Forget it. I need a drink with my friend."

"You're sweating all over. I'll get you a towel. Go in the lab, I'll grab another chair."

Julius raced to the kitchen and punched the air. Science hadn't advanced so much in the last five minutes that people could be in two places at once. And that purple light was a Magi Pod. He'd bet his Porsche on it.

He grabbed a towel and chair and rushed back to the lab.

The chancellor looked up. "No drink, then?"

God, they were good. His friend would say just the same.

"You of all people should know I keep a store in this fridge."

The chancellor closed his eyes. "Oh, right. The exercise addled my brain."

Julius grinned to himself as he took two beers from the fridge. This was almost too easy.

"I know you said you wanted to test out the new machine. I didn't realise you meant tonight."

"Uh, let's see it, then."

Julius wanted to study the face for concern but he had to play along, make this Maya comfortable … for now.

He took out the hypnosis machine and turned it on.

"The lasers work on your acupuncture points, and with my latest piece of genius—these electrodes on the wrist pulse—it only takes a few minutes."

He slipped the black band over his own wrist and adjusted the silver electrode under the band. He grabbed the white band and did the same to the chancellor.

"Put your other hand on the bench so we have a circuit." Julius picked up the metal pencil and placed it on the chancellor's hand.

The chancellor looked agitated.

"Don't worry," Julius said. "You can't get a faster way to lose weight."

The chancellor exhaled. "I sure as hell need something."

Teal hopped to the corner of the shed where she had hidden the Magi Pod. Standard issue to all Switchers, Magi Pods looked and acted like Ipods if picked up by an Earthie. You could communicate with anyone on Joya or Earth with a Magi Pod, and it worked like a mini-whiz laptop.

Teal saw the code appear on screen and downloaded the assignment: Operation Hector. She used the navigator on the Magi Pod and headed off to plan her mission proposal.

The Magi Pod suggested swimming across the river and entering at the bottom of the house there so she wouldn't be spotted. Teal headed for the front entrance. She only had an hour.

The house, as big as the Switcher Centre, stood in an acre of ground with a stable near the perimeter fence.

She rolled around in the dirt of one of the flower beds, rubbed extra in her face, and headed up to the house. She jumped up at the first window. The owner, Neville Parker, sat at the kitchen table with a photo in his hands. She couldn't see his face, but his shoulders shook. She jumped off the sill and snuck down to the stable.

Teal heard sniffs and a soft whine. She gulped. She'd never heard a horse cry. She wiped a paw across her face, gave herself a shake, and raced back to the shed.

Max sat in the corner of the condo while Teal paced. She had to help that horse.

But how? If they accepted her proposal, Zeus, champion Switcher, would join her as the other half of the team. He would know what to do in an instant. That's it! What would Zeus do?

Yes.

She ran the idea over and over in her mind and searched for holes. He would be proud.

The Magi Pod buzzed purple light. Teal leaned towards it.

"Testing, one, two."

"Testing *what,* you crazy rabbit?" Danny Loco's voice blared through the Magi Pod. "Open the transmission properly, or your proposal will be denied."

Teal kicked herself—which hurt with Jen's great feet.

"Opening address to the Maya Council. Switcher Teal, AKA Jen, requesting permission to put forward proposal."

"Permission granted. Proceed."

"Operation Hector," Teal said. "Four-year-old horse. Owner has given the horse no love or exercise since his wife died. Horse is distraught, and from what I've seen, the owner's unhappy himself, it's crazy, I don't know why he doesn't—"

"No sentiment," Hi Brid said.

"Right. Yes, sir." Teal bit her lip. "I propose Zeus and I meet the horse, check the facts, and forge a letter from a registered body on Earth threatening the owner. This will speed up the process and allow us to complete the assignment well inside the ten days."

"Under consideration," Hi Brid said. "Await verdict." The Magi Pod switched off.

Teal nibbled on a nail. She left Max on the ground floor of the condo and paced up and down on the first floor, the second, the third. One minute she congratulated herself on how well she'd done, the next she told herself off for letting Darcy down.

She dropped the Magi Pod and tripped over it. It buzzed purple light.

"Switcher identify," Darcy said.

Here we go. Teal took a deep breath and spoke into the Magi Pod.

"Switcher Teal, AKA Jen, awaiting results of deliberation."

"Switcher Teal, the decision is unanimous."

Teal's mind raced. Unanimous yes or unanimous no? Zeus had told her *Malcolm* gave the verdict. Darcy wanted to soften the blow. She couldn't stand it. Her head spun. She brought a paw up to her head.

"Teal," Darcy said, "your proposal has been accepted. Zeus and I will be on Earth within the hour to make the switch with the Earthie, Jon."

Darcy closed the connection. Teal felt as if a million jumping beans leapt up and down in her stomach. She'd done it! Yeeeehah! Teal the Switcher. They liked her plan! Oh wow, oh wow, oh wow!

Cool T looked at Julius. He'd nearly blown it not knowing about the fridge in the lab. He shook his head, drank his beer down, and felt his breast pocket for the Missing Memory Potion. He would have to get Julius to leave the room but at the moment he felt so relaxed. Hell, he could do with losing a few pounds.

Julius adjusted the lasers. Cool T blinked.

"Sorry," Julius said. "How's that?"

"Great," Cool T said. The lasers, or was it the thing on his wrist, made his body warm. He slouched and yawned.

"I conjure this reality," Julius said. His voice sounded far away.

Cool T scratched his head. He had something to do. He saw the lilac mountains through the window. He was on Joya … wasn't he?

Chapter 5

"I still think switching is for humans, cats, dogs, and ferrets," Hi Brid said. "Earth is dangerous for a rabbit." He raised his eyes to Darcy. She looked to the floor.

"Yeah," Freddie said. "Can't be easy adjusting to feet that size, man." The ferret raised his shades and winked at Malcolm.

Malcolm forced his feet through two orange cushions. He drooped his hands in front of his chest, hopped, then somersaulted, and landed on his bald head amid a roar of laughter.

"Destroying Maya Castle property is appropriate behaviour for a Council member, is it?" Hi Brid said.

Freddie lifted his shades, wiped away the tears of laughter. "Come on, lighten up. Malcolm´ll sew ´em up."

Darcy looked across at Zeus. He nodded, picked up his helmet and goggles, and they left for Earth to get the boy.

Part of Julius had thought—hoped—the Maya before him was Arabella, but it wasn't. She'd have recognized her own machine.

Julius never threw anything away, a habit for which he had never been more grateful. He smiled. The laser contraption had been stuffed at the back of one of the cupboards. Only now did he remember its use. The hypnotist—the one who wore the black band—created the reality in the other person's mind.

He said the words that transferred the thoughts. "I conjure this reality."

If this was Darcy in front of him . . . His nails dug into his palm.

"We're doing a mental evaluation on all Switchers," he said. "Standard stuff. Name?"

"Cool T."

So her highness couldn't waste her time to come and see him in person.

"Is Darcy Maya on Earth?" Julius's heart beat along to the throbbing in his head.

"No, she never switches now. Hasn't switched for twelve years."

What? Julius inhaled.

"As this is an intelligence test," he said. "What *would* make her switch?"

"Tough one." Cool T rubbed his chin.

Julius narrowed his eyes. "What if someone on Earth kidnapped one of her Switchers?"

"Ooh. She'd want to come down, but she doesn't do it. Joya Crisis Rule thirty-six: In the event of Earthie discovery, top four council members remain on Joya."

"Why?"

"They know our deepest secrets. Earthie politicians would exploit us."

Julius wanted to scream. He needed her in this lab.

"Something out of the ordinary," Cool T said.

Julius looked up.

"Maybe a few events to get her interested, and use the royal family. She loves them."

Julius leaned forward. "Do you think it would work?"

Cool T grinned and nodded. "Yeah, I do."

Jon brushed his teeth with his right hand as he inspected the bite mark on his left. He frowned. The rabbits had never bitten him before.

The last few days, it had been like Jen understood his every word. When she snuggled into him for a few moments, nothing else mattered. Jen had always been his favourite, but lately he couldn't get enough of her. Her paw had dug deep into his heart, unearthed a speck of the old happiness.

He noticed something fly past the window. He looked up, but too late. He rinsed his mouth and left the bathroom.

He walked into his bedroom, and his mouth fell open. His stomach lurched. A black-haired boy of about fifteen sat cross-legged on his bed. A Doberman stood on the blue rug. Instinct to protect his mother made Jon shut the door behind him.

The dog bowed its head. "We meet at last, Jon. I'm Darcy Maya." She offered her paw to shake Jon's hand.

He couldn't move. His back hard against the door stopped him from falling over. His head reeled. This dog spoke, smiled, and she knew his name! Was that a good thing or a bad thing?

Darcy Maya took back her paw.

"It's a good thing, Jon."

"You can read my mind?" Jon grabbed his legs to stop them trembling.

"Most people can. It's just training your mind to be more aware."

Jon looked over at the boy, who nodded and smiled.

"I'm Zeus," he said. "Come and sit down."

Jon wobbled over to the bed and sat up by the pillows, as far away from this Zeus and Darcy Maya as possible.

"You've been having dreams about us, haven't you?" Darcy said.

Had he created them by dreaming so much about them?

"We sent you those dreams so you wouldn't be too shocked meeting us today."

Didn't work very well, then, did it?

"Believe me," Darcy said. "You'd have been much worse off without the dreams."

Jon nodded.

"All you saw in your dreams is real footage from our planet, Joya. Not only does this lower the tension in the first meeting, it saves time, too."

"Do you really ride a motorbike?" Jon said. He loved motorbikes and had loved that dream.

Darcy nodded. "A Yamaha YZ400F. You'll be flying back to Joya on it with me in ten minutes."

"What?"

"Zeus here will be switching with you. He'll act as you for six weeks, and you'll come to Joya. Any questions?"

Jon had questions, all right. He flicked through the dream files in his mind.

"Is Joya really red and purple and shaped like a frisbee? Will I get to learn boxing? Do you really have sweets that don't rot your teeth?"

"Yes, yes, and yes."

"Wow! Hold on, though. He, I mean, Zeus—I mean you..." Jon looked to Zeus. "You don't even look like me. You've got black hair, you're older."

Darcy said, "Zeus will be blond, thirteen, and act like you for the duration of the switch. He's one of our best Switchers. Your mum'll have no idea."

"So, will I look like Zeus?" Jon asked.

"You don't change form. Only Switchers change."

"If I'm switching with Zeus, doesn't that make me a Switcher?"

Darcy laughed.

"No," she said. "Earthies who switch are called Traders. You don't change form, just swap places for six weeks. It prevents an imbalance."

"Six *weeks*?"

"We've got a lot to fit in. Your schedule is based around three key areas—opening your mind, self-confidence, and fun."

"Fun*?*"

"Yes. Keeps you healthy. You seem to have lost it."

Jon frowned. "Do I have to go to school up there?"

"On Joya we have Discovery, not school. You'll have none of the worries you have here, and our subjects are quite different."

Jon wondered how much they knew about him.

"Any more questions?" Darcy asked.

Jon shook his head. He didn't want to know.

"Right, belongings. You can take two things with you."

"Won't the things I take be missed?" he asked.

"No. We replicate them."

Decisions. He looked at the book he had to read for English and looked away. It had taken him days to get through the first chapter. Let Zeus try and get through it. Jon loved computer games yet couldn't decide on a specific game. No way would he take his football. It had been a year since he'd touched that thing.

"Jon, we need to get a move on."

He grabbed his dream catcher and his shark tooth fossil.

"Good," Darcy said. "Let's go."

Zeus passed Jon his helmet and goggles. He slipped them on and they fit perfectly. The helmet hissed and snuggled against his skull. He jumped. What the—?

"Impressive, eh?" Zeus said. "The special sensors adjust to any head size, and special probes feed into your skull to offset reduced oxygen pressure and stop blood building up in your abdomen and legs."

Jon shot a look at Zeus, then Darcy.

"Nothing to worry about," she said. "Stops any problems with altitude pressure. Once you get on Joya you're fine. The barometric pressure is like Earth's because of all the Maya dust."

Darcy's bike hovered outside the bedroom window. She leapt out of the window and onto the bike in one graceful bound.

Zeus gave Jon a leg up, and he found himself seated behind Darcy. He wrapped his arms in a bear hug around her. His dreams had shown him this bike didn't just fly, it did somersaults.

"Ready?" Darcy said. She revved on the accelerator with her right paw. The bike vibrated through Jon's legs. He looked back into his bedroom and gulped. Another him sat on his bed and waved. Jon shuddered.

Darcy sped off into the air. Jon closed his eyes and buried his face in her coat. After a few seconds, he looked down on Earth. His house looked like part of a model village. He loosened his grip around Darcy's chest. She let out a big breath.

"Fancy a loop?" she said.

Jon wanted to cling with all his might, yet he also felt safe. What the heck. . .

"First gear loop coming up. Lean forward with me."

I'm sure I didn't actually say yes.

"Loop!" Darcy said.

Whoosh! The bike lunged forward, then flipped them upside down.

Jon's stomach lurched toward his mouth. Phew, still on the bike.

"Okay, this time we'll do a double," Darcy said. "Remember to lean with me."

The first night of the human switch, the Maya Council had a welcome fancy dress party for the Trader in the Maya Castle. They played games and ate and ate.

Danny Loco looked around the Assembly Room and sighed. He ran a hand through his wild hair.

"Is it me, or is Darcy taking her time?"

Hi Brid looked at him. "Don't tell me, you're hungry."

"Can I help it if I get excited? I'm looking forward to meeting this Trader. He's smart."

"Let's start with Magi ball!" Malcolm kicked an imaginary football and did a back flip.

"Do we have to?" Hi Brid said. "It's so messy."

"Yes and double yes," Malcolm said. "Tom will love it!"

"Who's Tom?"

Malcolm wagged a finger. "Tut, tut, tut. Not like you, Hi Brid, to forget the name of a Trader."

"That might be something to do with the fact that his name is Jon, *not* Tom!" Hi Brid raised his eyes to the ceiling.

"Oh, right, yes, well, Tom, Jon sound similar, don't they?"

"Hmm. That or old age."

The Assembly Room doors opened. Freddie Maya, coolest ferret on the planet, strolled in.

"Hey guys, what's happenin'?"

"The ferret honours us with his presence," Hi Brid said.

"Ooh, still cheesed about the rabbit?" Freddie said.

"Where have you *been*?" Hi Brid said.

"Downloading some new tunes, man! Got to keep up with the latest vibe. Know what I'm sayin'?"

Hi Brid made a face. "Not a clue."

Malcolm laughed. Freddie turned to him.

"Malc, give me a beat." Malcolm, AKA The Human Beat Box, opened his mouth and started a hip-hop beat. Freddie began rapping:

> When Hi Brid ain't happy,
> He gets so snappy,
> What's the reason for this bad habit?
> Oh it's Teal, that pesky rabbit.
> Got no beef with cat, dog, ferret,
> For him the rabbit's got no merit.
> Teal's got the guts and the brain,
> It must be Hi Brid, he's gone insaaaane!

Everyone laughed and cheered. Freddie took slight bows, raised his shades, and gave a wink to a scowling Hi Brid.

"Just playin', H."

Hi Brid smiled despite himself and told everyone to finish the preparations.

Darcy and Jon emerged from the corkscrew funnel and catapulted through the sky. Jon screamed but nothing came out. He buried his head in Darcy's back.

"Welcome to our planet, Jon."

Jon lifted his head and gasped.

Lilac Mountains soared up to meet them from purple fields. Red roads snaked through the purple. Darcy slowed and Jon looked down to his right at rows and rows of stacked ring doughnuts.

"What are they?" Jon asked.

"Doughnut dwellings," Darcy said. "Like your apartments but no straight walls. Look left."

Four green glass pyramids rose to the sky in a semi-circle.

"Pyramid Plaza," Darcy said. "People in the top offices don't get much space, but their view is awesome."

Jon saw little figures seated at some turquoise tables in front of the pyramids.

"The Open-Air Café. Amazing milkshakes."

Darcy flew on and descended above a mass of red trees. The smell of strawberries shot up Jon's nose.

"Wow."

"Good, huh?" Darcy lowered the bike into the trees.

Jon expected to hear branches snap around them. He snuck a look and saw a shiny black stone path between a gap in the trees. Darcy touched down like a feather and didn't stir a single branch.

She rode down the path. The leaves shimmered on either side of them. Jon held out his arm, and his hand brushed through the leaves. His fingers felt wet and sticky. He brought them up to his face and licked the red juice. He'd never tasted strawberry so intense.

They emerged from the trees.

"Look ahead," Darcy said.

Jon stared at the huge purple stone building in the shape of a horseshoe. The four turrets had lime-green swirly tops like whipped cream, the same colour as the arched front door. Darcy pulled up.

"Off you get."

Jon lifted himself off the bike and looked up at the building.

"It looks good enough to eat."

Darcy jumped off the bike. "Lickety Split, Sixth Seat on the Council, has tried." Darcy raised her eyes. "Best girl we've had for decades but she licks things she likes. Chased by a policeman once in Italy because she ran off with a giant cardboard chocolate ice-cream, licking as she ran."

The bright green door slid into the wall on the right, and a jolly-faced old bald man in a pink ballerina outfit smiled at them. Jon couldn't understand how a muscly looking man with a tattoo on both upper arms would be a ballerina. The man looked down at his tutu and shrugged.

"I know. Only costume left. Anyway, you must be Jon, the new Trader. Good to meet you, mate. I'm Malcolm. Welcome to the Maya Castle."

He extended his hand, and Jon shook it.

"Darcy, your bath's ready," Malcolm said. "I'll take Jon to his den, give him the lowdown."

Malcolm led Jon into a golden entrance hall. Jon's mouth dropped open. His eyes soaked in the immensity. Malcolm turned left and Jon hurried after him.

"The stairs lead up to the kitchen," Malcolm said.

Jon's gaze followed the glass spiral stairs to the top.

Malcolm used his thumb to point out two deep red wooden doors on the left.

"Assembly Room," he said.

He led Jon down a twisty corridor and stopped in front of a black door with *Trader One Residence* painted on it in white. He handed Jon a red key.

"Open it up."

Jon opened the door. A big porthole window, directly in front of him, looked out onto a courtyard of turquoise daffodils. The giant navy blue sofa under the window would have taken up the whole of Jon's bedroom! He walked over and ran his hand over the peach skin fabric.

To the left of the sofa he saw a silver table with a navy blue chair tucked underneath. A gold circular laptop and what looked like a stack of games enticed Jon over.

"This is your den," Malcolm said.

Jon turned around.

"Through to the right is your bedroom, and to the left the bathroom." He pointed to the red doors on either side of the den. "Your wardrobe's full of clothes."

Jon looked to the left of the front door. In front of floor-to-ceiling mirrors, a black boxing bag hung from the ceiling, a pair of straps and blue boxing gloves draped over it.

"Your boxing training starts tomorrow." Malcolm tapped the bag. "Rocket Ron Johnson, the trainer, will expect you to practice here once he's shown you how."

Jon rubbed the side of his forehead. Malcolm patted him on the back.

"Don't worry, you'll love it. I'll leave you to get changed, you've got fifteen minutes. Your outfit's on the bed."

"For what?" Jon said.

"Darcy hasn't told you?"

"No."

"First night a Trader arrives we have a fancy dress party. You eat great food and play Maya games. We give you your agenda and everyone gets to meet you, see what they think."

Malcolm opened the door.

"But what if they don't like me?" Jon said.

"What's not to like? Anyway, we all had a nose at you while Zeus monitored you. Professor Danny Loco thinks you're clever. Can't miss him, black hair all on end. Best scientist on the planet. Only sixteen."

Malcolm left the room. They liked him. Professor Danny Loco—what a name. He went to change for the party. His party.

Darcy paced her den.

"Come on, Cool T, you should be back by now."

A knock at the door made her jump.

Cool T stood at the door in sunglasses. She stood aside so he could enter.

"Any problems?" she asked.

Cool T shook his head. "I put the potion in his beer."

"Did you see him *drink* it?"

"Even watched him crush up the can when he finished."

Darcy sighed. "I owe you."

"No problem. Kinda fun doing something illegal for our leader."

Cool T bowed, and she laughed.

"What's with the shades?"

"I've got a helluva headache. He had this laser machine in his lab and I accidentally looked at one. I'm gonna miss the Trader party. Just want to get to my den and sleep, okay?"

She nodded and grabbed her costume for the party.

Julius Webb looked out of his lab window up into the sky and laughed. The Maya had left thinking he'd given Julius the

Missing Memory Potion. Instead, Julius had messed with a Maya mind. How did *they* like it? Darcy would be next, and he wouldn't be so easy on her. Not so easy at all.

His great mind formed a plan within the hour. The queen was old, the chancellor a jerk, and the prime minister—well, that couldn't be helped. PC Frank Willis would be his errand boy. Julius's eyes glazed over. He could taste vengeance on his tongue.

Petlandia closed at nine. He needed to leave now.

Chapter 6

Zeus stood in Jon's bedroom and talked to himself in the mirror. He practiced Jon's expressions. The interested tilted-head look, the shocked look, the adorable son look. He blinked, leaned his head back, and his clothes changed into a replica of Jon's blue and white pyjamas. They hung from Jon's slim frame. Jon would benefit from the boxing training, no question.

Zeus heard Jon's mum coming up the stairs and leapt into bed.

The attractive woman he'd watched on the Blib—thick dark hair, olive skin, green eyes—walked into the room.

"I thought I heard voices up here," she said.

Zeus threw her the interested tilted-head look.

"You must've been talking in your sleep again."

Zeus rubbed his eyes and nodded.

Jon's mum kissed him on the cheek.

"Goodnight, son."

"'Night," he said, through a yawn.

She closed the door and went downstairs.

Zeus let out a breath. He wanted to congratulate Teal but he had to wait until Jon's mum went to sleep.

After an hour, to keep himself awake, he slipped out of bed and began shadow boxing in front of the mirror. One-two, jab, jab.

Jon's mum called up the stairs, "Are you all right up there, Jon?"

Farts!

"Uh, yes. Weird dream, that's all. G'night."

He crawled into bed. Darcy would go ballistic at his carelessness. He'd have to see Teal in the morning. He knew she'd be cheesed, but he couldn't risk it.

Teal paced up and down the top storey of the condo.

"I know I shouldn't expect so much from such a great Switcher—after all, who am I? First time Switcher, never been on a mission before, I understand, and I'm just a rabbit and—"

"Enough!" Max said. Teal's mouth fell open.

"I think you're a great rabbit," Max said. He picked a piece of leaf out of his teeth.

"You do?" Teal puffed out her chest.

"Yes, when it's not all about *you.* Why isn't Zeus coming to see you? Why can't you stay out in the garden all night?"

Tears welled up in her eyes.

"This self-obsession is sooo boring," Max said. "Zeus voted for you, didn't he?"

"Yes, but—"

"How about you losing the word 'but' from now on. Think you could do it?"

Teal wiped her nose with a paw. "Why?"

"It's lazy," Max said. "Sounds like a moan, or a lie."

Mmm. She always said to her dad, "I did, *but* ... " and after Rocket Ron's workouts, "I want to train, *but* it's so hard." Urghh, she hated whiners.

She had a thought.

"So when I asked my cousin to run through boxing techniques with me and he said, 'I would, *but* I have homework,' he lied."

"Not necessarily."

"But you said ..." Teal threw her paw over her mouth.

Max smiled.

"I said it can sound like a lie. Most of us like it straight, Teal. Say it like it is."

"I understand bu—" Teal huffed at herself. "Wouldn't you upset someone, being so direct?"

"No. It takes a while to get used to leaving it out, and it's worth it."

Teal narrowed her eyes and rested her chin on a paw.

"Let's practice," Max said. "Ready?"

Teal took a deep breath, put on her concentration face, and nodded.

"Will you take me back to Joya?" Max said.

"I'd love to, Max, but you know I can't."

Max frowned. "Not a great start, Teal."

"But you know I can't take you to Joya, you could go there but only on a switch, I don't have the power, I wish I did, but I don't."

"That's three buts in four sentences."

"But I'm explaining."

"Four."

"Bu—"

Max looked up to the sky and counted to three.

"You could've said *I don't have the power to take you back to Joya with me* or *Sorry Max. Only the Maya Council can make a decision like that.* Both these sentences are nice and the truth."

"Okay, got it," Teal said. "Do I have to say sorry, though? It's not easy for me." Understatement of the year. She couldn't remember the last time she'd said sorry. Had she *ever* said it?

Max twitched his nose.

"It's only hard if you make it hard. Sorry is just a word. What does it hurt to use it? I guess if you can't say it, though ..."

Teal raised her paws. "Okay, okay. Let's have another go."

"Umm. Okay, got one," Max said. "Can you spend the day with me tomorrow?"

Teal winced at the 'S' word. She had no choice. If someone said she couldn't do something, she had to rise to the challenge.

"Sorry, Max. I have to go through the assignment with Zeus, then meet Hector, the horse. When I'm finished we can play."

"Well done!" Max ran around in circles. Teal grinned.

They carried on practicing half the night.

Julius shut the lab door, looked around at his three purchases, and smiled. The corgi whimpered as Julius doubled the white band around its paw and slipped the electrode underneath. The poodle and the parrot watched from their cages.

"I conjure this reality," Julius said.

He visualized the corgi being hugged and kissed by the queen, felt the charge pass through him into the dog. The corgi closed its eyes and lay down.

"Bite your new owner," Julius said. "And she'll love you forever." He repeated it over and over.

He slipped the band and the electrode off the corgi's paw and moved on to the poodle.

All three pets, desperate for happy homes, hung on to Julius's every word.

He loaded a syringe with the deadly truth serum. He didn't care if their owners threw them out after that first bite. The job would be done. A nip would stretch the pores and allow the saliva containing the serum to pass through.

He smiled. The pet owners' truths would steal the headlines and lure Darcy to Earth.

Jon looked in the mirrors around the boxing bag and frowned. He'd rather have stayed in his pyjamas than wear this costume. He heard a knock at the door.

He opened it, and a chocolate brown ferret strolled in.

"I'm your chaperone, Freddie Maya. Call me Freddie." He raised his paw.

Jon had never seen a real ferret before. As for a talking one, wearing shades?

"Give me a high five, man."

"Oh, right," Jon slapped his hand on Freddie's paw.

"Yo, bro. Nice outfit."

Jon shifted from one foot to the other. He looked at the football kit in the mirrors. It was number nine, Joe Canter, voted best player of the year. He bit his lip. At least they couldn't make him play.

"Like your den, then?" Freddie said.

Jon nodded. "I love it."

"Designed it myself. We like to give you Traders a den that fits."

"Wow. Thanks," Jon said.

"No problem, man. Lets walk and talk or we'll be late. Gotta grab my costume on the way."

They made their way down the twisty corridor.

"What are you going as?" Jon asked.

"The Fighting Ferret. Boxer. Easy outfit to move around in. Boxing shorts, robe, boxing boots."

"What about the gloves?"

"No way, man. I won't be able to eat the chow with gloves on."

Freddie's costume lay on a chair in the golden entrance hall, and he put it on.

Darcy walked into the hall dressed in a leather flying jacket, cap, and goggles.

"Yo, Dawg," Freddie said, and raised his paw. Darcy slapped it to the side. Freddie wobbled from the force but managed to stay standing.

They all laughed and walked over to the doors of the Assembly Room. Darcy barked and the double doors opened.

Jon's mouth dropped open. Silver minerals coated the ceiling. The walls, decorated with stick-on stars, made the room look like a sky. Rainbow-coloured glitter floated in the air.

Jon bounced on the yellow spongy floor and looked at all the giant brightly coloured cushions scattered over it. A long sea green table in the shape of a series of waves carried a feast of multi-coloured fruit, meat, cheese, and chocolate on its peaks and dips. Bottles of water spilled over a giant two-tiered ice bucket.

A man with long black hair dressed as an Indian warrior sat on a giant purple cushion. He looked like an Indian too. He gave an air of importance with his chin protruded and his nose raised in the air.

Malcolm did back flips in his tutu and Jon laughed.

A teenager with black hair standing on end and black lines painted on his face, dressed in black boots and combat gear, walked over. He clicked his heels together and saluted.

"Professor Danny Loco at your service, sir."

So this was Danny Loco.

"At ease, soldier." Jon grinned and saluted back.

Danny Loco laughed.

The Indian warrior stood up.

"Everyone feast!" he said.

Danny took food from one of the high crests of the waves, Freddie stretched up to one of the dips. Jon picked up a plate and stacked it with cherries, chocolate, and chicken.

The three of them sat on some red cushions, and Freddie and Danny Loco gave Jon the lowdown on everyone.

"Malcolm," Danny Loco said.

"The ballerina, man," Freddie said.

"Exactly. He's an expert acrobat, gymnast, boxer, and sews like an art. A real people person. Everyone loves him."

"Sewing?" Jon could imagine Malcolm on a rugby team, not holding a needle.

"That's right." Malcolm walked up to them, heavy-footed for someone in ballet slippers. "Got a problem with that?"

Jon shook his head. Who would? Malcolm looked tough even dressed as a ballerina.

"The native American is Hi Brid," Freddie said. "First Seat on the Maya Council, most powerful man in the room. That handsome big black guy dressed as a policeman is Rocket Ron Johnson, boxing trainer."

Jon looked across at the policeman and gulped.

"All ready to address the Trader," the Indian said. He rose from his green cushion. "I'm Hi Brid, First Seat on the Maya Council. The Maya Council and all Maya beings welcome Jon the Trader to Joya."

"Here, here!" Danny Loco yelled.

Hi Brid scowled at him, then walked over to Jon and handed him a book.

"Your agenda," Hi Brid said. "You've arrived late. You should have read it by now. Don't let the four hundred pages put you off."

He patted Jon on the shoulder and walked away.

Jon looked at the book and groaned.

Darcy stood and raised a paw to Jon.

"Darcy Maya, Second Seat on the Maya Council. I'll ensure your schedule is adhered to. Welcome on behalf of all Dyad Mayas."

Jon whispered to Freddie, "What are Dyad Mayas?"

"Super Switchers," Freddie said. "Human Switchers change into Earthie humans, animal Switchers into Earthie animals. Dyads—or Super Switchers—change into any human or animal we want."

Jon stared at Freddie. "You're a Super Switcher?"

"Yep. So's Darcy and Lickety Split. All of us with Maya at the end of our names."

The immense black policeman eased himself up from a yellow cushion, his muscles bursting to escape from the uniform.

"I'm Rocket Ron Johnson, boxing trainer extraordinaire. I'll have your head buzzing and your muscles screaming."

Jon grimaced.

"Professor Danny Loco," Danny jumped up. "Fourth Seat on the Maya Council. My role is to aid your learnings." He saluted and clicked his heels. Hi Brid raised his eyes to the ceiling.

Malcolm stood up.

"Malcolm the Sugar Plum Fairy here." He did a pirouette and everyone roared with laughter.

"And these are *top* council members," Hi Brid buried his head in his hands.

Malcolm laughed and continued. "Third Seat on the Maya Council and best acrobat on the planet." He went up on his toes, put his hands over his head in a ballet pose, and did a double back flip. Everyone cheered.

"The Sugar Plum Fairy thanks you all," Malcolm waved like the queen. "My role, Jon, is to help you discover fun. I now hand the floor to the wonderful, the talented, the great, the poetic . . . Freddie Maya."

Freddie threw off his boxing robe and stood in his red and white shorts and red boxing boots.

Malcolm produced a drumbeat from his mouth and Freddie began rapping.

> All in the house, don't be quiet like a mouse,
> Let's make some noise, for this here boy.

Everyone shouted, "Yo, yo, yo!" and Freddie began shadow boxing.

> Jon's the latest Trader, we've all made a wager,
> What will he learn, before his return?
> Malcolm's bet a penny, the lowest of any,
> Loco's bet the most, and he likes to boast,
> That this here Trader is one clever dude,
> Eats information just like it was food.
> Sure looks cool in his kit, number nine,
> I'm outta here, show respect for the rhyme.

Jon cheered with everyone else, desperate to hear the song again.

Hi Brid raised a hand. "Okay, let's get down to business, Jon. You Earthies come to Joya for two reasons. The first you know: to enable us to swap places with you and accomplish good things on Earth."

Jon nodded.

"The second is for you to overcome obstacles that hinder your happiness."

Jon looked at the book. Four hundred pages didn't make him happy.

"We tackle your issues head on—as you may have guessed." Hi Brid nodded at Jon's football kit.

Jon shook his head.

Hi Brid walked over and placed a hand on Jon's shoulder. Jon looked into those brown-black eyes and saw only kindness.

"Face it," Hi Brid said. "And it falls away."

Jon bit his cheek.

"You'll see." Hi Brid squeezed Jon's shoulder, then nodded to Freddie.

"Okay," Freddie said. "Bring on the games! Magi Ball first."

Malcolm grabbed a ball that looked like a normal football except it seemed to be breathing. Jon frowned. Football. The cause of all his problems. He relived that missed penalty and hung his head. They couldn't make him play.

Danny Loco ran over and took Jon's book. "I'll put it in a bag by the doors," he said. "It's gonna get messy in here."

What?

"The ball's filled with Danny Loco specials and Maya dust," Freddie said. "Has a personality all of its own, man. You kick the ball and shout the name of the person you want the ball to go to, or shout what you want to come out of the ball.

"If you shout a name, that person gets the ball on the head, but no one knows what the ball will fire at them. If you shout what you want the ball to fire, the Magi Ball chooses who it goes to. Everyone knows *what* will be squirted, we just don't know who's gonna get it."

Malcolm placed the Magi Ball in the centre of the room, and everyone formed a circle around it.

"Games and sports, everything you do, should be fun," Malcolm said. "And you don't get much funner than Magi Ball."

Jon stared as the ball rolled around on its own. It stopped in front of Malcolm, who screamed in excitement, then rolled on and stopped at Freddie Maya.

"Hi Brid!" Freddie shouted.

If Jon didn't know better, he could have sworn the ball smirked. Freddie kicked the ball. It did three loops in the air and headed across the circle to Hi Brid, who bit his lip. The ball landed on his head and WHOOSH! out poured a bucket of custard all over his head and down his shoulders.

Everyone cheered and laughed. Jon couldn't believe the ball had the courage to do that to Hi Brid. He covered his grin with a hand.

"After you've been hit," Freddie said, "the ball lands at your feet for a second. If you're quick you can shout a request and kick the ball." Hi Brid, too busy scooping cold custard out of his eyes, missed his chance.

The ball rolled around the room once more and stopped at Rocket Ron Johnson.

"Jelly and cream!" Rocket Ron kicked the ball.

The ball didn't make it easy to guess and pretended to stop at a few people. It chose Malcolm and crashed down on his head. Malcolm immediately shouted, "Horse poo!" and kicked the ball before it had a chance to roll off.

There were shouts of, "Urrrrrghhh," "Disgusting!" "Yuck!" Malcolm laughed and licked the black cherry jelly and cream as it ran down his face.

The ball danced in the air and hovered over Danny Loco's head. He closed his eyes and brought his hands up to his face, but the ball moved. It flew over to Hi Brid and burst over his head. Hi Brid wiped his face and looked furious. People either side of him tried not to screw up their faces at the smell.

The ball didn't wait but span around the circle. This time it stopped in front of Danny Loco. "Darcy Maya!" he yelled and kicked the ball.

The ball landed on Darcy's head and covered her with sea water. She spat out a bit of seaweed. "Malcolm!" she yelled as she kicked the ball.

The ball flew through the air and hovered above Malcolm's head as dry pasta rained down on him. He didn't get filthy, but it looked a bit painful.

The ball rolled again and stopped in front of Jon. He felt all eyes on him. His toes tingled. Malcolm put a hand on his shoulder.

"Come on, mate. Do it for you, for fun."

"Gunge!" Jon shouted, and kicked the ball. Malcolm and Freddie grinned and nodded as the Magi Ball flew into the air. It hovered over Hi Brid, who gave it a warning scowl. Yeah, right, like the ball cared?! It flew across to Rocket Ron and released litres of thick, green, slimy liquid over his head and shoulders.

Everyone shouted, "Uggggh!"

Rocket Ron said, "Professor Danny Loco!" and kicked the ball.

It zoomed across to Danny Loco and covered him in spaghetti sauce. He licked a bit off his face, shouted, "Cold porridge!" and kicked the ball.

Jon grinned and itched to get the ball back.

They played Magi Ball all night—with the exception of stinky Hi Brid—no one wanted to stop. The game got messier and messier.

Jon and Freddie squelched back to their dens. Jon, with bits of potato and cabbage in his hair and sticky from honey, licked the back of his hand every now and again. He loved honey. He carried the bag with his agenda in the other.

"You know what, man?" Freddie said, covered in syrup and feathers amongst other things. "I look like a ficken or a cherret."

Jon laughed. He hadn't laughed, or played football, for so long. It felt good.

Chapter 7

Frank Willis walked up Julius's drive and studied the dark red paving underfoot. Mosaics of eagles and falcons adorned the path. The dusky pink beasts stood out against the deep red. Frank reached the door, knocked, and looked right at the green garage door. He shook his head as he remembered driving Julius's Porsche with the windows rolled down.

Julius opened the door and handed Frank a coffee. "Thanks for coming round so early."

"No problem." Frank took a sip. "So, did your ex read the paper?"

"Huh? Oh, I don't think so." Julius led him through to the lab.

Frank shielded his eyes. "What's this, a laser show?"

"Sorry. An experiment. Slip that white band and electrode over your wrist and wrap up the cord, will you? I'll take this one and then I can switch it off." Julius pulled a black band over his own wrist.

The electrode felt warm against Frank's skin.

"I conjure this reality," Julius said.

"What?" Frank stifled a yawn. He felt so warm, so cosy.

He took another slurp of coffee, then smiled. He'd never had such a great friend. Julius nodded, as if he had read his thoughts. He slipped the band off Frank's wrist."All done."

Frank's senses heightened. Blimey, he could run a marathon. *Some* coffee. He gulped down the rest.

"I have three special presents I need delivered this morning," Julius said. "I want someone I can trust to do the job. I can trust you, can't I?"

Frank puffed out his chest. "Of course."

"I need a holiday. I'm going around the world. I leave in an hour."

"*What?*"

"*You* said I should get away."

He had, at that. Or at least he remembered saying it now. Julius handed him a key.

"I'll be away for three months. I thought you could look after it for me."

Frank stared at the key. "The *Porsche?*"

"There's a present for you under the front seat. You helped me more than you realise. I'm giving all my friends a present to celebrate my retirement." Julius placed a hand on Frank's shoulder. "It's just money. I didn't know what would be your perfect gift."

Frank shook his head. "I can't accept it, Julius."

Julius grabbed Frank's arm. "You sorted me out. That would've cost a small fortune with a psychiatrist."

Frank grinned and stuck out his chin.

"You'll need the money anyway. That car's costly to run. Agreed?"

Frank nodded. What a friend, and he's famous!

"The pets are for the queen, the chancellor of the exchequer, and the prime minister," Julius said.

Frank didn't know what to focus on first: the Porsche, the pets, the queen.

"*Pets?*"

Julius nodded. "I've got the queen a corgi, the chancellor a parrot—he loves anything tropical—and a poodle for the prime minister. His died a few months ago. The pets are in the car in the garage."

"In the *Porsche?*"

Julius nodded. "The windows are open." He gave him letters for each delivery. "You're sure you don't mind?"

"What are friends for?" Frank said.

Julius grinned.

Zeus opened the shed door as Teal was teaching Max to smile. Teal swallowed her smile in a second.

"Sorry."

Zeus shook his head. He introduced himself to Max. Teal couldn't hold her excitement.

"Oh my gosh, Zeus, we had the most amazing night. Do you notice anything different about me? Do you? Do you?"

"Well, your feet are bigger. You're still hyper, Teal, that's for sure. Let me think, is there anything else ..."

Teal tapped her hind foot.

"Well, if I'm not mistaken," Zeus said, "I think I actually heard the word 'sorry' come out of your mouth."

Teal and Max gave each other a high five.

"Yes, yes!" Teal said. "My black and white friend here taught me some amazing things."

"Looks like you've taught *him* some things. Earthie rabbits do high fives, do they?"

"Ah, yeah, sorry about that. Max got me to say sorry," she said. "And it's not that bad, after four hours' practice last night, it isn't even painful any more."

Zeus laughed.

"Sorry, sorry, sorry. See? Easy peasy lemon squeezy. Oh, I almost forgot, I've stopped saying the word BUT, because people think you're lying or something when you use it."

"I'm astounded," Zeus said. "Great proposal, by the way. I wanted to come and congratulate you last night but nearly got found out."

Teal gasped. He could have jeopardized the mission.

"Jon's mum's in London today so let's make the most of it," Zeus said.

"Great, once we meet the horse we'll know what we're up against, better to research first."

"Blimey, Teal, steady on. At this rate you'll get a Gold Bean from Hi Brid."

Hi Brid sent Gold Beans to Switchers who achieved ´beyond the norm´. The Gold Bean contained handwritten congratulations from Hi Brid, a high prize indeed. *Zeus* only had one. Teal, the first rabbit ever to receive one? Wow.

"Let's go." Zeus waved. "See you later, Max."

"Bye, Max!" Teal ran after Zeus.

They swam across the river behind the house. Teal, used to the warmth of the Unfathomable Lake, shivered in the icy river.

She jumped over the perimeter fence with no problem, but Zeus slipped and got his T-shirt caught. It ripped. He landed with a thud and yelled. He looked at the piece of T-shirt stuck in the fence and groaned.

Teal shot a glance up at the house. "Come *on*!" She ran for the stable, Zeus right behind her. They crouched and waited.

"Who's there?" Neville Parker shouted as he opened the back door of the house. "I have a gun and I shoot people who trespass on my land."

He waited for a minute then went back inside.

"Phew. Sorry, Teal," Zeus said.

The horse, Hector, got the smell of them, started neighing, and scratched his hoof on the stable door. Neville Parker flew out of the door, shotgun over his arm, and ran towards the stable.

They're hunters down here. They hunt us. Teal's stomach churned. Mr. Parker would have rabbit and Zeus pie. They both looked at the hay box to the left of the stable. Zeus grabbed Teal, threw her into the box, and dived in after her.

"I see you!" Mr. Parker shouted. Their hearts came up in their mouths.

He walked over to the hay box and dug the butt of the gun into the hay. He missed Teal by a whisker. Zeus squeezed her paw.

"Come on out. I know you're in there."

Neither Teal nor Zeus moved.

"Okay."

He cocked his gun.

Hector heard the sound of the gun being cocked, and it spooked him. He broke out the stable door and bolted towards the house. Neville Parker swore to himself, spun around, and ran after the horse.

Zeus grabbed Teal by the scruff of the neck and jumped out of the hay box. They shot over the fence and into the river.

From under the water, Zeus and Teal could hear Mr. Parker's muffled screams.

"I'll get you next time!" he yelled.

They waited until their breath had run out, then burst out of the water like two torpedoes, coughing and spluttering. Mr. Parker had gone back into the house.

Frank Willis reached under the driver seat and pulled out a cardboard box with his name on it. He opened it, and fifty pound notes burst out. He counted *thirty* thousand pounds. Something nagged in Frank's mind, but he couldn't concentrate. He ran his hand over the leather of the passenger seat. He wouldn't tell his mother about the money.

His first stop: Buckingham Palace. Frank spoke with the guard, who made a call.

"Drive straight in, sir. Her Majesty is expecting you."

Frank's stomach lurched. He hadn't thought he would *meet* her.

The queen stood outside the front door, talking on her mobile. She beckoned him with her free hand.

He got out of the Porsche, grabbed the corgi, and walked up to the queen.

She put her hand over the phone.

"Oh, how thoughtful of Julius," she said. "Could you hold on a moment while I end this call? Then *do* come in and have some tea."

Frank had no idea how to address the queen, let alone sit and have a conversation with her. "Uh, I'm sorry, ma´am. I have a busy day." He handed her the lead.

The queen nodded and continued with her phone conversation. Frank drove off, cursing his fear and lack of etiquette. He checked the rear view mirror and saw the corgi bite the queen's ankle.

The next stop: 11 Downing Street. The first police guard recognized Julius's car, raised his hand to wave, then stopped. Frank handed him the note, and the policeman radioed ahead for him to pass through.

Frank grabbed the parrot cage and knocked on the door. The cleaner answered.

"The chancellor is otherwise engaged, sir. May I take the gift?"

Frank handed over the parrot.

"Otherwise engaged, otherwise engaged," it squawked.

The cleaner blushed. Frank hid a smirk and went back to the car to get the poodle.

The policeman on the door of Number 10 took the poodle for the prime minister. Frank returned to the Porsche and sank into the seat. He had done everything Julius had asked of him.

Darcy paced her den unable to sleep, Julius Webb filling her thoughts. The room erupted in white light, and she squinted. In'Lakesh stood before her. The lilac beam from the unicorn's horn flickered.

"Nothing will be helped without rest," In'Lakesh said.

"You told me I had reason to worry," Darcy said.

In'Lakesh blew through her nostrils. "I meant for you to take action, not pace and race your thoughts."

"Don't mince your words."

"I won't," In'Lakesh said. "Get some sleep." The unicorn closed her eyes to show Darcy how.

Darcy tried, but the memory kept jolting her awake. The moment when she caught them that night. The hatred in his eyes. Arabella wincing as Julius crushed her hand in his, forbidding her to take a step towards Darcy.

Arabella had told Darcy later Julius frightened her, his love for her so intense, so greedy. Darcy had never feared an Earthie before. She shuddered. She owed Cool T, big time.

Jon woke up to the most disgusting smell: himself! So tired last night, he had fallen into bed in his football kit without showering off the honey and other mess from the evening's festivities.

He tried to pull the quilt back but couldn't. It had glued itself to his skin. He panicked, thrashed around in the bed in an attempt to free himself, and ended up looking like a human hotdog in a quilt bun.

He decided to drag himself and quilt into the bathroom. He part hopped, part jumped across the bedroom and fell flat on his face into the main room of the den. He inched his way across the floor like a caterpillar, sweating by the time he reached the bathroom.

He knelt and flipped the shower lever on with his head. He didn't have much room until the water saturated the quilt and he could peel it away. The walk-in shower didn't allow for a person wrapped in a quilt.

The gunk from the Magi Ball and the quilt clogged up the drain, and water seeped out of the shower. The quilt looked like a deflated swimming pool. Jon went to get dressed before he cleaned the bathroom.

Chapter 8

Jon sat on his sofa and opened his agenda. Four-*hundred* pages. He rubbed his forehead, shut the book, and looked through the computer games.

Someone pounded on the door and he jumped.

"Yo, bro, I overslept," Freddie said. "Open up, man, we're late."

Jon opened the door.

"Morning, Freddie Maya," Jon said.

"Hey. What I tell you last night, man? Don't be getting all formal wi´ me. Freddie or FM. Slap the paw."

Freddie raised his paw, and Jon slapped it to the side.

"What the …?" Freddie said.

Jon saw the water seep under the bathroom door into the den.

"Oh, no—I went to bed in my clothes, woke up with the quilt stuck to me. I took it all in the bathroom and showered it off. It must have plugged up the shower."

"Been there, man, worn the sticky T-shirt. First time I played Magi Ball? You know what Malc is like, obsessed, man. Got me covered in jam, syrup, you name it. I hit the sack in all that goop. By morning even the pillow stuck to my head. The bed all red, thought I'd sprung an artery. Then I realised. I ain't never been so relieved to see strawberry jam, man."

They both laughed.

"I need to sort out the bathroom," Jon said.

"No time, bro. Gotta fly. Your agenda says you got boxing training, and Rocket Ron Johnson don't accept late arrivals. My fault, man, I couldn't get out of bed this morning. Darcy'll skin a ferret when she finds out I got you there late. My Magi Pod's goin' off." He pressed the mini Ipod hanging around his neck.

They stepped outside the castle, and Malcolm shook his head at Freddie. He stood next to a mini red and black Harley Davidson. Jon wanted to stroke it. Lickety Split would put this on her Lickable List for sure. Freddie ran up the back tyre, onto the seat, and told Jon to get on.

"Are you mad, FM?" Malcolm said. "Jon won't fit on your bike. You should've been here half an hour ago. Lickety Split waited as long as she could."

"Damn," Freddie said.

"Darcy'll go ape when she finds out you haven't left yet."

A tall dark-haired man on a quad bike drove out of the giant garage and grinned.

"I'll take you both. Nice to meet you, Jon. I'm Cool T, Lickety Split's dad."

Jon smiled and said hello.

"Freddie, get on the seat behind me," Cool T said. "We'll fly, it's quicker. Jon, your feet slot into those footrests on the back. Hang onto the rail behind me."

Jon stood on the quad bike.

"Am I strapped in or anything?" he asked.

"No need. The footrests have static suction. All Maya vehicles have it so you can't fall off. If you take your hands off the hand rail, you could fall backwards and break your neck or your back. But your feet will stay attached to the quad. My advice, don't let go."

"Thanks, I feel much better."

Cool T sped into the air. Jon held on for dear life before he realised the hand rail also had the suction mechanism. He couldn't let go if he tried.

Cool T laughed.

"Very funny," Jon said.

Jon got off the bike outside the gym and swayed like a tree in a breeze.

"Take deep breaths," Freddie said.

The two of them walked up to the door.

"I don't feel up to boxing training." Jon rubbed his hand across his stomach.

"No choice, bro. Rocket Ron accepts *no* excuses. With Teal's carry-on too, you're already behind schedule."

"Who's Teal?"

"No time. Tell you after. Two important things to keep on Rocket Ron's good side, and believe me, you don't want to be on his bad side. Know what I'm sayin'?"

Jon gulped and nodded.

"First, be on time, so we've already cheesed him off this morning."

Jon groaned.

"Second, push yourself. If he sees you're slacking, he'll make you suffer huge."

Freddie opened the door of the gym.

"Pick you up in an hour," he said, and walked back to Cool T.

What? Jon looked over his shoulder. He'd thought Freddie had training too.

Rocket Ron Johnson scowled.

"My copy of your agenda says nine-thirty. *Why* are you late?"

Jon glanced at the others sitting on the gym floor and wished he could be any one of them. He didn't know what to say. How could he be mad at Freddie when he hadn't read his own agenda? He gulped and took responsibility.

"I don't have an excuse. I'm sorry. It won't happen again."

"Darn right it won't! Everyone's doing ground work. There's no time to introduce you. The tongue *may* be the strongest muscle, but it's the least used in this class. Understand?"

Rocket Ron pointed to a girl with blond plaits and a happy face.

"Partner Lickety Split over there."

She waved. Jon, excited to meet her, didn't dare speak.

"Right," Rocket Ron said. "I want sixty up and overs. The person holding the feet counts for the other person, then change. Jon, as you've neglected your football training for over a year, we'll just have to hope you can do half."

Blimey, tell the world, why don't you?

Lickety Split lay on the floor with her knees bent and her palms on her thighs. Jon looked at the others and grabbed her feet the same way.

"Time!" Rocket Ron said.

Lickety Split began doing super fast sit-ups. Jon forgot to count. As she came up each time she reminded him, "seven, eight, nine," and he took over.

Lickety Split finished first. She sat up, pushed Jon down, and grabbed his feet. He started doing the sit-ups, but Rocket Ron screamed at him.

"Jon! The hands stay on the legs at all times and go *over* the knees."

Easy for you to say. Jon cleared his mind in case Rocket Ron could read his thoughts.

At thirty up and overs, Jon struggled. His stomach burned, and Rocket Ron told him to stop. Lickety Split put her hand on Jon's knee and smiled. His body tingled.

Rocket Ron shouted, "Alternate elbow sit-ups, then change to vampires when I say."

What? Jon had no clue. Lickety Split lay down, hands at the side of her head. Jon looked around the room. He copied the others, wrapped his arms around Lickety Split's knees and sat on her feet.

Rocket Ron called time, and Lickety Split and the others began doing sit-ups. Jon counted forty-two when Rocket Ron shouted, "Vampire! I want fifty, then change."

Lickety Split, like the others, placed her hands on opposite shoulders like a mummy and did sit-ups. She did fifty.

Jon found the vampires excruciating. His stomach screamed after the four he managed. How quickly he had gotten out of shape.

"Gloves and pads!" Rocket Ron shouted.

Lickety Split ran and got some pads, then put them on Jon. She put on her gloves and held her hands to her face in a defence position.

"Okay," Rocket Ron said. "Throw a jab, then a one-two. Time!"

Lickety Split hit Jon's pads and nearly knocked him over. Rocket Ron came running.

"Jon," he said. "When the boxer's about to throw, be firm on your feet and keep the pads still. Like this." He gave a demonstration. "Move *between* shots, keep your boxer moving. Understand?"

Jon nodded. He had never paid so much attention in his life.

He didn't think things could get worse until he had to swap to gloves. He couldn't take in all the terminology: jab, hook, parry, counter. His mind and body had nothing left by the end of the session. Rocket Ron could have been saying "throw an orange" for all he cared. He wanted to lie down. For a year!

CIA Agent Shatner landed at Heathrow Airport, London, his thoughts focused on Julius Webb. He didn't believe the retirement story and he needed that truth serum.

He walked through arrivals and his old friend greeted him.

"Shatner. Long time." Chief Burns held out his hand.

"Burns. Good to see you." Shatner gave Burns a half hug, half handshake. They made small talk until they got to the car and Burns started the engine.

"How long am I putting you up for?"

"A few days," Shatner said. "Anything hot been happening this side of the pond?"

"Nothing much. Except—keep it to yourself—a couple of my idiot officers arrested Julius Webb."

"The scientist?"

"Exactly. All a misunderstanding but then he wouldn't leave the cell. I had to let him go. He's friends with the queen and the PM."

Shatner nodded and stared into space.

"So, why are you here?" Chief Burns asked.

"Hmm? You know the drill," Shatner said. "Security. Let me do my job. I may need to use you, though."

"Nothing changes."

Jon stepped on the quad bike behind Freddie and Cool T. Every muscle ached.

"In your state, better not to fly," Freddie said.

"Cheers." Jon gripped the quad as Cool T sped off. Red dust came up around them.

"All sessions with Rocket Ron are tough," Cool T said. "The first few are the worst."

"Great." Jon had no energy to speak.

Freddie looked over his shoulder. "My first session, my legs collapsed from under me."

Jon could well imagine.

"I curled up on the gym floor, pulled my towel over me, and fell asleep. An hour of hell, man, I'm tellin' ya."

Jon closed his eyes and enjoyed the breeze blowing over his face and arms.

"Here's the Funky Fountain," Freddie said.

Jon stepped off the quad.

"I'm giving a lesson at Discovery," Cool T said. "See you guys later."

Jon and Freddie waved as Cool T flew into the air.

"What do you think of the fountain, man?" Freddie asked.

Jon turned around and his mouth fell open. Rainbow-coloured water erupted from the top of a double-peaked mountain. The water flowed down its sides and settled in the circular moat, where it turned to thick liquid gold. Stone armchairs, adorned with thick yellow cushions, encircled half the fountain.

"Wow!" Jon stretched his arms—and grimaced.

"Don't worry, man," Freddie said. "Get some of Hobo's hot chocolate in you, you'll feel better."

They walked around the fountain. A bright pink and brown van with *Hobo's Hot Chocolate* written on the side stood amongst some deep red oaks in a park of purple grass that spread forever. The smell of rich chocolate seeped into Jon's nose and encouraged his legs to move faster.

A tall man with large brown eyes stood in the van, dressed in pyjamas. His long grey hair lay in a ponytail down his back. Jon and Freddie watched him work.

He broke up enormous bars of rich dark chocolate and put them in a red pot the size of a bath. As the chocolate melted, he poured in litres of soya milk, a giant bag of raspberries, and a smaller bag of cherries. He whipped the delights and mixed in two spoonfuls of one powder, then two cupfuls of another.

He dipped a finger into the mixture, popped it into his mouth, and closed his eyes.

"Hobo's our planet shaman," Freddie said. "There's not a spirit here who won't talk to him, and he can heal anything with that chocolate of his. Yo, Hobo! How's it goin'?"

Hobo opened his eyes. "Busy. Started at five this morning, haven't had time to get dressed."

"Well, this new Trader's no exception, man. Give him the Choco Works. Had his first session with Rocket Ron. Give me one, too. I've had me a grillin' from Darcy."

Jon shot a look at Freddie.

Hobo threatened Freddie with a chocolate ladle. "What you been doin' to upset Darcy?"

"Overslept," Freddie said. "Set the new Trader up for a bad first boxing session. Deserved all I got. Still, comes tough after a rockin' party with the Magi Ball."

Hobo shook his head.

"I don't envy anyone a first session with the boxing freak, and to be *late?* No wonder Darcy's mad." He looked at Jon. "You okay, man?" He passed him a Choco Works and sprinkled some extra powder on top.

"Yes, thanks, just tired. I've never done anything like it."

"Nobody ever has, son," Hobo said. "I've put some extra Maya dust on top. You need it."

Jon took a sip. His tongue told his brain heaven had arrived. He wiped his mouth with the back of his hand. "This is fantastic," he said. "Like drinking velvet."

"Hmm," Hobo said. *"Want something smooth? Drink velvet. Hey, Freddie,"* He handed the ferret a Choco Works. "Can you and Malc record a little something for me tonight?"

"Sure," Freddie said. "Any excuse for a bit of studio time. Come on, Jon, let's lift the legs by the fountain."

"Lift the legs?" Jon asked, between mouthfuls.

"Take a seat, man."

Freddie jumped up onto a stone armchair, and Jon sat next to him. Freddie pointed up at the Funky Fountain.

"All the Spirit Guides meet here. Mine spends more time here than with me."

Jon heard a roar as the water erupted. A gorilla appeared out of the top of the fountain and beat its chest. Jon struggled not to spill his chocolate.

"Unlike you, Freddie," the gorilla said, "we have the ability to be in more than one place at the same time. I never leave your side."

"Joke, Hercules," Freddie said.

The gorilla closed his eyes and dove back into the fountain.

"Sensitive." Freddie put his drink down beside him.

"Wow. Are they all gorillas?" Jon asked.

"No. Humans, animals, birds. You *saw* Hercules?"

Jon nodded.

"Impressive. You met your Spirit Guide?"

"Didn't know I had one," Jon said.

"An Earthie can have loads, man. We tend to have one each up here."

Jon gazed up at the top of the fountain. "I wonder what mine looks like."

"Ask at Discovery," Freddie said. "There's a meditation you can do to meet them."

Lickety Split walked over from the other side of the fountain.

"Not too tired to have a Choco Works, Jon?" she said.

Jon wiped his mouth and straightened his T-shirt. "Uh, thanks for reminding me about counting the sit-ups."

"You're welcome." Lickety Split frowned at Freddie. "I hear someone got a telling-off from Darcy."

"News flies on this planet," Freddie said. He stretched out his legs and put his paws behind his head.

"Well, I don't know if you know the facts. You got this Trader to boxing late, and *he* took the blame for you."

Freddie leapt up on the armchair and looked at Jon.

"Don't know what to say, man." He lifted his shades onto his head.

"Thanks?" Lickety Split said.

"Yeah, 'course. Thanks. That's huge to do what you did, man." Tears of gratitude welled up in Freddie's eyes.

Lickety Split laughed.

"Best rapper on the circuit, and soft as cotton wool."

"Ain't nothin' wrong with showin' a sensitive side."

"Too right," Lickety Split said. "That's why we all love you."

"Seen my new bike?" Freddie asked.

"That gorgeous red and black Harley? Frogs and dogs! That's some machine." Lickety Split's eyes glazed over. "It called to me like a red, juicy apple. I had to lick it."

"Be offended if you hadn't, girl!"

Freddie and Lickety Split's Magi Pods buzzed purple light. They read the message, "*Maya Castle, now!*"

Chapter 9

Freddie and Lickety Split looked at each other and shrugged.

"Who knows?" Freddie said. "Can you give us a lift back?"

"Sure. Ever ridden on a rocket, Jon?" Lickety Split said.

Jon stopped his face from contorting and shook his head.

"Come on, it's just like riding a metal horse. Has static suction in the air like all the vehicles, you can't fall off."

The rocket whooshed through the air, and the force shook Jon's cheeks. The adrenaline rush was terrific.

Malcolm stood at the entrance of the Maya Castle. Freddie, the first off the rocket, asked why they'd been summoned.

"Something's happened with Teal and Zeus," Malcolm said.

They entered the Assembly Room, and the voice-activated Magi screen buzzed purple light.

"Opening address to the Maya Council. Cordial civilities to all in attendance. Switcher Zeus, AKA Jon, downloading information on operation to date."

"Proceed," Darcy said.

"Problem has occurred on first day. Apologies. I unnerved the horse before making contact, fell off the fence. The owner came out with a gun—"

"A *what?*" Darcy said. "This is supposed to be a straightforward mission for a first-time Switcher. We don't send rookies into situations with guns." '

Jon looked at all the worried faces in the room. Zeus continued.

"I take full responsibility and ask for permission to hand leadership over to fellow Switcher Teal, AKA Jen, sir," Zeus said.

Hi Brid shot to his feet. "And you think she is capable, on her *first assignment*, to be the *chief* Switcher?"

"I do. Without doubt, sir."

Hi Brid paced the room. Everyone looked at him.

"Closing connection for consideration."

Jon looked at his finger. Teal had swapped places with Jen. *Teal* had bitten him. And it had been Teal snuggling up to him, making him feel better.

Hi Brid spoke.

"I have never—*never*—heard anything so ridiculous in my life."

"What part do you find ridiculous?" Danny Loco asked.

"ALL OF IT!"

"Zeus wouldn't put the proposal forward if he didn't think it feasible," Lickety Split said.

Hi Brid said, "I think, my dear girl, that anything is possible right now. For all I know, Zeus has been switched with someone from another planet, and that isn't Zeus we're talking to."

"Ah, just to point out," Freddie said, "we're the other planet. So that ain't likely."

Hi Brid scowled at him and turned to Darcy.

"Well?"

"I think Zeus is tired," Darcy said.

"Oh, that's all right, then. Zeus is tired, accidents happen …."

Darcy raised her eyes.

"Look, if I'd known about the danger, I would never have chosen it as Teal's first mission. We should bring her back."

"I agree," Hi Brid said. "Should never have sent a rabbit, especially after—"

"I disagree with both of you," Malcolm said.

Freddie nodded. "I second that."

"What?" Hi Brid clenched his fists.

"Not only is Zeus a respected member of the Council," Malcolm said, "but he also comes from a long line of great Switchers."

"Spare me the history lesson, get to the point," Hi Brid said.

"My point *is*, a suggestion from someone of Zeus's calibre deserves our consideration."

"He's right," Freddie said. "Zeus wouldn't suggest something so out of the ordinary unless he had good reason, man."

Hi Brid shuddered.

"You think a rabbit—*Teal*—is capable, do you?" Hi Brid spat across the room.

"We should consider the proposal without prejudice," Malcolm said. "Those in favour?"

Hi Brid shook his head. An hour later everyone had agreed except him. Darcy called for a two-hour recess.

At 11 Downing Street, London, the Chancellor of the Exchequer devoured his favourite meal—ten sausages and a mound of mashed potatoes. His body filled the sofa. With a fork in his left hand and a pen in his right, he signed off papers as he ate. He heard a squawk and looked up.

A gold metal cage sat on top of the walnut bureau at the far end of the room. A parrot with a yellow head and green body pecked at its feathers. The gift from Julius! His housekeeper had told him, but he'd forgotten all about it.

He smiled, heaved himself from the sofa, and walked over to the cage.

"Hello, you beauty, do you speak?"

The parrot tilted its head to the side. The chancellor poked a podgy finger into the cage, and the parrot grabbed it in its beak.

"Ouch!"

Malcolm, Freddie, and Jon left the Maya Castle.

"Let's walk to Hobo's," Freddie said. "I need the fresh air, man."

They headed down the black stone path amid the strawberry-leaved oak trees. Jon breathed in the intense flavour. Malcolm took a heart-shaped leaf in his palm, squeezed the sides, and opened his mouth. Jon copied, and the red liquid poured into his mouth. Malcolm smiled.

They emerged from the trees, and Jon looked up at an enormous bar of chocolate—at least four metres high. A few chunks had been replaced with red framed windows. Hobo opened the two-chunk door.

"Come on in," he said.

They entered the lime-green hallway, inhaled the aroma of melted chocolate, and followed their noses to the kitchen.

Dark red cupboards ran the length of the wall on the right. The left wall had been replaced with a giant bar of chocolate. Jon wondered if you could eat it. The wooden table in the middle of the room had red armchairs of different heights around it. On the table, a golden tray overflowed with an array of fruits drowned in chocolate.

"Help yourself," Hobo said. "Strawberries are my favourite."

Malcolm grabbed a chocolate-dipped strawberry and took a bite.

Jon and Freddie both took apple slices. The combination of sharp apple and sweet dark chocolate filled Jon's mouth with liquid. They all grabbed more and sat around the table.

"Why the mass exodus from the park today?" Hobo asked.

Malcolm looked at Freddie, who shrugged.

"Keep it under your hat, Hobo," Malcolm said. "Seems we have an emergency change of leadership with Teal and Zeus."

"What? Impossible. It's Teal's first switch."

"Yes, well, we have a meeting back at the Castle, so we need to get a move on."

Hobo rubbed his chin. "This is why the Spirit Guides are agitated."

"What do you mean?" Freddie asked. "What have they said?"

"That I'll be called at the end, that it may be too late."

The three of them looked at one another.

Jon wished he could read minds. Too late for who?

Hobo looked at him and jumped up.

"This new Trader here has a great slogan for my drinks, *It's like velvet*. I want to record something to play through the van speakers."

Hobo pressed a button under the table, and the chocolate wall dropped underground to reveal an enormous recording studio. Jon nearly choked and spat out a piece of orange.

Hobo laughed. "Impressive, huh?" He patted Jon on the back.

"Give me a beat, Malc," Freddie said. "I got somethin'."

Malcolm started with his drums. Freddie jumped onto the table and began rapping:

> Hobo's got the choc-o-late, listen to me,
> Gives you a na-tu-ral high, lusciously.
> The drink's so smooth, so listen how I tell it,
> Hobo's hot cho-co-late, feels like velvet.
> Wanna dive right in,
> Pour it on your skin,
> 'Cos it's like velvet, baby,
> It's like velvet.

Freddie rapped the first part, then sang the last four lines.

"Love it, Freddie," Hobo said. "Let's record it."

Jon's mind wandered back to what Hobo had said. Too late for who? For Teal?

"Hey, Jon," Hobo said. "You're making quite an impression."

Jon looked up.

"Overcome your crazy stubbornness about football already *and* protected Freddie."

Jon shot a glance at Freddie, who raised his paws.

"Not me," he said. "The Spirit Guides—mine included—tell Hobo everything."

"Come on," Malcolm said. "We better head back."

They left with a tin of chocolate fruits.

At 10 Downing Street, the prime minister sat on his bed. He stroked his moustache and frowned at his wife.

"I think you could at least agree to *see* the dog," his wife said. "She's very sweet."

The prime minister folded his arms and pouted.

"If I'd wanted another dog, I would have got one. Julius should've asked me. What would my little Chequers think?"

"That you're childish and cruel to *this* dog," his wife said, pointing to the door.

The prime minister continued the argument as his wife opened the bedroom door. The little white poodle sat with head low and eyes sad.

The prime minister rubbed his forehead and went to the poodle. He scooped her up in his arms, went and sat on the bed, and stroked her. The poodle bit him.

"I don't want a dog that bites, dear."

His wife tut-tutted. "More like a friendly nip. Look at her now."

The poodle gazed up into his eyes, her head cocked to one side. The prime minister's eyes filled with tears and he pulled the dog into his chest.

"Chequers," he said.

Freddie put his paw on the lime-green arched door of the Castle. The door hummed and glided into the wall on the right. The three of them walked into the golden entrance hall, and Malcolm reached into his pocket.

"Almost forgot." He handed Jon an orange marble. "Your Blib."

"Blib?" Jon ran the marble around in his palm.

"Blow on it," Freddie said.

Jon blew. An orange light poured out of the marble and lit up the ceiling.

"Put it between finger and thumb and direct it at the wall."

Jon took the marble in his other hand and pointed it at the wall. Five metres of the gold wall glowed orange.

"Blow again," Malcolm said.

Black writing appeared in the orange light: *New Blib message.* Jon looked from Freddie to Malcolm, and they both used their eyes to direct him back to the wall.

His rabbit Jen appeared before him in 3-D. Jon's eyes widened as she began to speak.

"Hello, Jon, I'm guessing if you've opened this, then you've already met some animals that talk. My name's Teal, I've swapped places with your rabbit for six weeks."

She raised her forepaw and bit a nail.

"Uh, I didn't mean to bite you, I got frustrated 'cos I couldn't help with Pigbreath, you're a great person and I hope we're friends, you've already got a big place in my heart.

"Anyway, I'll be leaving messages on here to keep you updated on what's going on, you can record *me* a message if you like … if you like.

"I hope they're not too hard on you up there with your learnings, have a good time. Love, Teal."

The image disappeared. Jon smiled.

"She bit you?" Freddie said.

"Not hard, she only wanted to help." Jon closed his hand around the Blib and smiled. "She did help."

"Come on," Freddie said. "I'll show you how to record a message later." He pointed to the Assembly Room doors. "We need to get back in there."

Jon slipped the Blib into his pocket and they walked over to the doors. They heard Hi Brid and Darcy's raised voices.

"A human would never send a *rabbit* to do the work of a cat, dog, or ferret."

"What are you saying?"

"Fight! Fight!" Malcolm said. Hi Brid and Darcy looked around. "Our two most *mature* members of the Council?"

Jon hid a smile and then noticed a phantasm of a wolf sat beside Hi Brid.

Hi Brid looked from his wolf to Jon and frowned. Jon didn't know if he should have seen it.

"Are we doing this or not?" Darcy said.

Jon looked around the room.

Darcy turned to the screen. "Activate." A flicker of purple buzzed over the surface.

"Switcher identify," she said.

"Switcher Teal, AKA Jen, awaiting decision over leadership change."

"Teal, the decision has been made," Darcy said. She looked at Hi Brid. He shrugged, closed his eyes, then gave a slight nod.

"You are appointed Chief Switcher."

A gulp echoed through the Magi Screen.

"Zeus," Darcy said, "I shouldn't have sent you on back to back assignments. Have the day off school tomorrow. Be sick."

"Jon's mum will suspect," Zeus said.

"Well, you'll have to be convincing, then, won't you? You may not be Chief Switcher any more but I want you back on top form to protect Teal."

"Understood," Zeus said.

"Good. Make the most of the rest and sleep tomorrow. You'll need it."

Everyone except Hi Brid shot a glance at Darcy. She bared her teeth and they all looked down.

"Put Teal back on for daily learnings."

"Learning one," Teal said, her voice a little shaky. "*Sorry* is just a word, saying it can be like giving a gift to someone, so why not?"

All council members´ mouths fell open. Malcolm recovered first.

"An important learning. It'll make your life easier. Any more?"

"One. The word BUT is a lazy word. It can be misinterpreted as a lie or an excuse. I took it out of my vocabulary and have noticed how much that improves communication and lessens misunderstanding."

Malcolm grinned at Darcy.

"You can spot a great Switcher in a monstrous mudstorm!"

"How have you discovered such important learnings?" Hi Brid asked.

"Max, the other rabbit here. He knows everything."

Jon shook his head. Amazing.

"Utilize this Earth rabbit," Darcy said. "Good luck, Teal. Closing transmission."

Malcolm passed around the chocolate fruits and looked at Hi Brid.

"What?" Hi Brid said. "Did I say anything?"

"No," Malcolm said. "But now you have, what are your thoughts?"

"I'm shocked," Hi Brid said. "The rabbit may be growing up." He popped a chocolate covered cherry in his mouth and spat the pip into his hand. "I think all Mayas should start implementing these new learnings."

Freddie grabbed a chocolate covered raspberry. "I can't imagine Rocket Ron saying sorry in the gym, man."

Everyone laughed.

"Maybe we start with the council members," Darcy said. "Some of us will find them tough!"

Freddie nodded and turned to Jon. "It's late. We're outta here."

Jon followed Freddie out of the Assembly Room and down the windy corridor. Freddie explained Blib recording on the way. They stopped outside Jon's den.

"Charge your Blib in your laptop," Freddie said. "I'll be here at ten tomorrow. More boxing training, and your first day at Discovery."

Jon's mind raced from the Blib, to boxing, to Discovery. He turned to ask Freddie a question and saw the ferret disappear around the corridor.

Jon turned the key in the door and walked in. Someone had cleaned the den. He went over to punch the punchbag and noticed a piece of paper stuck to it.

Floods on your first day?! I sorted your room. From now on, it's down to you. Darcy does spot checks. Be warned!
Malc

Jon took out his Blib and held it in front of himself.

"Record," he said. The Blib beamed red light above his head and showered his body in red crumbs.

"Hello, Teal," Jon said. "Thanks for your message and no problem about the bite. It's nice to know you wanted to help me—and you did. We're definitely friends."

He smiled and gave a thumbs up with his free hand.

"Hope you're enjoying Earth. It's amazing here, but I guess you know that already. Does Max speak? Say hi to him for me. G´nite, friend. Send."

Jon brought the Blib to his lips and blew on it. The light went out.

He opened the laptop and put the Blib in the indentation marked Blib Recharger. The marble filled with an array of colours and purred like a cat.

Zeus came back into the shed after supper. Teal paced the ground floor of the condo as Max snored on the top floor.

"How you feeling, Chief Switcher Teal?" Zeus said.

Teal shook her head and held a paw over her tummy. "Shocked. Hobo must have hypnotized Hi Brid, or he's up there spitting feathers."

"I know," Zeus said. "He can't help it. Don't take it personally, Teal. He's traditional."

"Racist."

"A little closed-minded."

"Whatever. He's right, though, I shouldn't be Chief Switcher. I'm a rookie, what if I fail?"

"We haven't spent this many years getting rabbits in the system for you to mess it up, girl. Hi Brid needs to see greatness to be persuaded, and greatness he'll see."

She wished she had Zeus's confidence.

"Hey, catch." Zeus threw the orange Blib, and Teal caught it in her paws.

"I've got a message?"

"Mmhm. I can't believe you bit him."

"Zeus, that's *my* message."

"Joys of sharing a Blib"

Teal played the message.

132

"I can't believe he still likes you," Zeus said.

Teal beamed.

Zeus walked back into the living room, the TV blaring. Jon's mum lay on the sofa, still in her suit, holding the remote control across her chest, and snoring.

Zeus slumped in the armchair. He'd wanted to be Teal's fellow Switcher, to help her. And what had happened? He nearly got her killed! He shook his head. The news began and he looked up.

The queen has made a shocking announcement. At an official opening in Brighton, Her Majesty announced that she is sick of being queen.

Zeus laughed. Yeah, right. The queen appeared on the screen.

I am the most antisocial person I know and would rather stay at home with a good book instead of meeting the general public. The reason I wear gloves is because I don't enjoy touching the sweat of the common people.

What the ...? Zeus sat on the edge of the sofa. The newsman returned on the screen.

Experts are suggesting her majesty may be overdoing things and in need of a rest.

Zeus glanced at Jon's mum still sleeping. He ran out to the shed.

Chapter 10

Darcy ran through the monthly figures with Hi Brid. The Assembly Room doors opened. Malcolm cartwheeled over to them.

"Enough with the accounts," he said. "I've got an idea."

Hi Brid and Darcy looked at each other.

"Why don't we have a trapeze in here for people?"

"*People?*" Hi Brid said.

"Hey, if I'm flying around up there, I'm not bothering you with cartwheels down here."

The voice-activated Magi Screen buzzed purple light.

"Switcher Zeus, emergency transmission."

Darcy closed her eyes.

"Proceed," Hi Brid said.

"Unusual human behaviour to report. The queen's said she hates her job. Says she doesn't like the common people, or what they might contaminate her with."

"*Which* newspaper is this in?" Hi Brid asked.

"I saw her say it," Zeus said. "On the news."

Darcy saw a flicker of concern run across Hi Brid's eyes.

"Thanks, Zeus." She closed the connection and looked from Hi Brid to Malcolm.

"I'm going down to find out," Darcy said. "I'll have a word with George, see if he knows anything."

"George as in *Prince* George?" Hi Brid said.

Malcolm looked at Darcy.

"He's an adult now. You don't know how he'll react."

"Malcolm, something's going on and ..." Darcy started to mention Julius Webb but stopped herself. Malcolm could read her mind, and she didn't need any sarcasm from Hi Brid.

"Tell me what other choices we have?" Darcy said. "Any other person, fair enough. However, this is *not* normal behaviour from the queen of England. I don't want to wait around on this. If I go and see George—"

Danny Loco strolled in. Hi Brid, Darcy, and Malcolm all looked at Danny, then to the ground. Darcy rushed out of the Assembly Room before he could read her thoughts.

Jon woke to the football alarm. He threw it off the bedside cabinet and stumbled out of bed. He got dressed and went to his laptop. The Blib glowed orange, and he picked it up.

"I'm charged and holding a message," it said.

Jon grinned. He blew on the Blib twice and faced it towards the wall. *NewBlib Message* projected onto the wall amid orange light.

Teal appeared in 3-D in front of him.

"Hello, Jon. Thanks for your message. I played it over and over."

Jon grinned.

"Max can speak—only to me and Zeus. He's full of information, I'm learning loads, wouldn't it be great if we could be down here together and work on an assignment?"

Jon nodded.

"Zeus's looking forward to school, Pigbreath won't be expecting one of our champion boxers in your skin—don't mention that to Rocket Ron, by the way.

"Have to get on with my assignment, have a great day, friend. Love, Teal."

Jon folded his fingers around the Blib and went and sat at the silver table. Max speaking! He shook his head. He wished he could be with Teal, but he also wanted to be on Joya, and he was happy to wait until Zeus dealt with Pigbreath.

He had seen two Spirit Guides and might find out how to meet his today. He closed his eyes and imagined a giant rabbit.

He heard a tapping and looked at the door. Underneath, he could see a flashing red light. He put the Blib back in its charger.

He opened the door and jumped back as a giant red jelly bean flew past him. It circled the den a few times and started shouting.

"Bulletin Bean! Bulletin Bean! Bulletin Bean for Jon the Trader!"

It landed on Jon's agenda. He looked at it but stayed a safe distance.

"Come on, man!" the Bulletin Bean said. "Open me up. Places to go, people to see."

Jon picked it up as if he had a porcupine in his hands. It opened in his palm like a box with hinges, and a note flew into the air. Jon grabbed the note and put the Bulletin Bean back on his agenda. He read the note.

Yo, Jon,
What's happenin'? Chasing my tail, man, so no time to come get you. Cool T's gonna take us to boxing. Meet you out front at five to nine.
Freddie.

The Bulletin Bean spoke:

"Close the Bean, I'm outta this scene!"

Jon picked up the Bulletin Bean and closed it. It leapt out of his hands and flew out of the den, shouting, "I gotta fly, saying bye-bye!"

Jon laughed and waved at the Bulletin Bean. He looked at the shark-tooth clock, pulled on his trainers, and left the den.

Cool T sat on his quad outside.

"Morning, Jon. Hop on. Freddie's on his way."

Freddie emerged from the red trees on his Harley. He pulled up beside them.

"Hey, guys. Howz it goin'?" He yawned, stretched, and fell off his bike.

"Better than you by the looks of it," Cool T said. "You all right?"

Freddie nodded. "All-night session." He ran up the quad and sat behind Cool T. "Let's go, man."

Darcy flew down to Earth. Should she turn up at Prince George's as herself or as a person? Would he remember her? If anyone stood by the dream laws it would be him. She took a chance.

She picked the lock on the back door and walked in. She entered the sitting room and saw Prince George stretched out on a sofa, his head buried in a polo magazine. He glanced over and jumped up.

"What the—" He rolled the magazine and raised it above his head. A light of recognition flickered in his eyes.

"*Darcy?*" he asked.

Darcy nodded and sighed.

Prince George rubbed his eyes. "So the dreams—"

"They all happened. They've stayed with you. Remarkable adherence to Joya learnings. Well done."

"Crikey." Prince George scratched his head. "So your being here, does that mean I get to go again? Are you still flying a motorbike? What are you riding now?"

Darcy raised a paw. "We're troubled by the news about your grandmother."

"I know, she's beside herself." Prince George sat back on the sofa. "She doesn't know what made her say it. She cancelled all her appointments today. She *never* does that."

Darcy had to ask but didn't want to go where the answer would lead.

"George, does your grandmother know the scientist Julius Webb?"

"They're friends. Why? Is he all right?"

"He's retired, hasn't he?"

"Yes. He gave Grandmother a present to celebrate, a new corgi."

Darcy closed her eyes. Julius had regained his memory, she could feel it in her fur. She should have checked he'd taken all the potion, should have known better than to trust Arabella in her condition. But Cool T said he'd watched Julius drink it.

Cool T landed in front of the black, windowless building. Freddie and Jon jumped off the bike. Jon stared at the red rocket-shaped sign above the door, *Rocket Ron's Gym*.

"Know why he's called Rocket?" Freddie said.

Jon shook his head. He didn't have a pointy head or anything.

"He had a fight, threw an uppercut so hard, so fast, the man took off in the air like a rocket. Can't catch him. I'm tellin' ya. Super fast."

"Is Lickety Split coming to training today?" Jon said.

"No, man. Haven't you read your schedule?"

Not unless he meant the first page.

"Today you're on your own with The Rocket."

"I have to fight him?" Jon heard his voice squeak.

Cool T laughed. "Nah. You've got an hour, not two seconds."

The door of the gym opened. Rocket Ron Johnson smiled down at them.

"Isn't punctuality a beautiful thing? Shows respect, my gran always used to say." He looked at Freddie and raised his eyebrows.

"Hmph. Pick you up in an hour, Jon," Freddie said. He muttered under his breath, "Oversleep, just the once …"

Jon and Rocket Ron walked into the gym. Jon put his straps and gloves on.

"First things first," Rocket Ron said. "Never, and I mean *never*, use boxing outside of the gym, unless it's self-defence. Understand? If I find out you have, even when you're back on Earth, I'll come and sort you out myself."

Jon thought of Zeus with Pigbreath. Zeus was a champion boxer. It wouldn't be self-defence. He shook his head and filled his mind with images of throwing the jab.

"Want to get on with the jab, eh?"

Jon's head jerked up to Rocket Ron. He gasped.

"Don't worry, Jon. I like to see that someone with talent has his mind focused."

Talent?

"Okay, don't let it go to your head."

Rocket Ron brought his hands up to his face.

"First, defense. Always be on a side angle. Right-handed boxers like yourself are called orthodox. As an orthodox, your left foot should be forward and your left shoulder facing your opponent. That way, they've only got half a target. Like this."

Jon copied the stance.

"Now at ALL times, you have to have your guard up."

Jon caught a glimpse of himself in the floor-to-ceiling mirrors. He thought he looked pretty good.

"Now, those mirrors you're admiring yourself in," Rocket Ron said, "are there for a reason. You see yourself when you're shadow boxing. Fast way to improve yourself is to watch for what's weak and work on it."

Rocket Ron put on some pads.

"Give me a jab. For an orthodox, that's a left punch, quick and sharp." He demonstrated a lightning jab. Jon didn't see a thing. Rocket Ron slowed it down.

"Hit the pad, then get that glove back to your face. Remember, step *into* the jab."

Jon threw jabs until his left arm burned.

Rocket Ron walked over to the black boxing bag and threw a one-two.

"You have mirrors and a bag, right?"

"Yes, sir," Jon said.

Rocket Ron showed him how to work the bag.

"Okay, now let's see a bit more power."

Jon nodded. He imagined his dad's face on the bag, and the jab flew out of him.

"Whoa. I'm glad I'm not your dad. Give me a one-two."

Jon punched the bag again and again. Rocket Ron had him rest for thirty seconds between rounds. His arms and shoulders burned.

"Okay, stretches, then you can go," Rocket Ron said.

Jon no longer needed to cover his thoughts about Zeus. His mind had enough to think about: *protect yourself at all times, see what's weak and sort it, I have talent, I have talent ...*

Teal woke up at first light and headed over to see the horse.

She shivered as she entered the lake—what she wouldn't give for a dinghy. She shook out her fur at the other side, jumped the fence, and went to the stable.

"Hi, Hector."

The horse opened one eye. Then the other. He let out a breath, and his jowls shook.

"Down here."

He glanced down and saw Teal.

"What on Earth?"

Teal raised a paw to silence him.

"Let me explain why I'm here, then you can neigh the house down if you want. Agreed?"

He nodded. "I've never spoken to a rabbit before."

Teal sat back on her haunches and put her forepaws on her hips.

"Well, in case you hadn't noticed, *you've* never spoken before."

"Oh!"

"I'll tell you why I'm here, then you can chat away."

"I'm all ears." He pricked them up.

"My name's Teal, I'm a Maya and come from a planet called Joya, we come down to Earth to help out Earthie animals and humans, you're my first mission, an L.O.L and an N.E."

Hector tilted his head to one side and raised a brow.

"Lack of Love, Need Exercise," Teal said.

Hector hung his head.

Teal felt tears prickle in her eyes.

"It's not your fault, Hector."

She moved forward, raised a paw, and stroked Hector's leg. The leg flew towards her. She swayed back and jumped in the air at the same time. His hoof scraped her cheek, and she landed flat on her back.

"Are you okay?" Hector said.

Teal swayed as she stood and steadied her head with her forepaws.

"You kick people and then ask if they're okay?"

"Reflex reaction. My right front leg's ticklish, sorry."

Teal rubbed her jaw. She should be getting paid for this.

"I've written this letter to your owner." She cleared her throat and recited it from memory. She'd been up half the night writing and rewriting it.

> Dear Mr. Parker,
> It has come to our attention that, as owner of the horse, Hector, you are not abiding by the wishes of your late wife.

Hector sniffed. Teal looked up at him and continued.

Our animal auditors have noted your lack of attention
to the horse and are deeply concerned over the absence
of exercise. Mrs. Parker assured us that you would
keep your promise to her.

Hector broke down.

"Okay," Teal said. "I don't need to read it all, you get the
gist." She bit her lip. "What do you think?"

Hector sniffed. "I miss her."

"I know. So does he. This will remind him to do the right
thing by you."

Chapter 11

Cool T, Freddie and Jon pulled into the Maya Castle garage. Jon's mouth dropped open. Two rockets gleamed to his left, another quad at the far end. Three motorbikes stood in a line to the right. An electric blue surfboard hung on the wall.

He followed Freddie and Cool T out of the garage and up to the front of the castle.

Freddie put his paw on the lime-green door, and it slid sideways.

"Joy, Danny Loco's mum, does lunch Tuesdays," Cool T said. "Gets her Monday morning blues a day late, so she cooks and dances salsa to keep them away."

"At the same time?" Jon said.

"Yep. Releases her happy endorphins."

"Right mess in the kitchen, man," Freddie said. "But she's a helluva cook. Eat well, stay well, know what I'm sayin´?"

Jon followed them up the glass spiral stairs off to the side of the entrance hall.

Cool T opened the door. Salsa music and laughter burst out to greet them. Aromas from Indian spices glided up Jon's nose. A woman danced around a gold oven in the centre of the immense kitchen. Her long dark hair flew all over the place, as did the curry on the spoon she waved high above her head. Her jeans and blue blouse had splats of curry and flour all over them.

The back right half of the kitchen had a half-moon stage with floor-to-ceiling amps, a drum kit, keyboards and some mikes. Eight giant armchairs and matching beanbags, as white as toothpaste, surrounded a burgundy dance floor.

The back left half of the kitchen grabbed Jon's attention. Lickety Split sat at the back of four sloped rows of green velvet chairs, a quest game playing on the cinema screen. She bashed away on the giant arm rests, and *new winner* appeared on the screen. She raised her fist in the air, took off her interactive headset, and looked around at Jon.

"Hey, Jon," Malcolm said. "So you're off to Discovery after lunch."

Jon brought his eyes back to the first half of the kitchen. Malcolm sat next to a boy who had his head in a book. They sat at an oval lilac table encircled with purple seats of different heights. Cool T sat down the other side of Malcolm.

"Thought you'd be here," Malcolm said.

Cool T rubbed his stomach and grinned.

Freddie ran up a stool and sat opposite Cool T. Jon sat next to Freddie.

"Introductions, Freddie?" Joy said, brushing some flour off her cheek.

"Sure," Freddie said. "For everyone who hasn't yet had the pleasure, this is Jon the new Trader. Gifted, too. He saw my Spirit Guide."

Everyone's eyes widened at Jon. His face got a bit hot as Lickety Split sat next to him. Freddie continued.

"Jon, that wild woman cooking the chow and dancing the salsa is Joy, Danny Loco's mum. We call her Joy 'cos she's so happy. Real name, Arabella."

"Pleased to meet you," Jon said.

"Ditto." She smiled all the way up to her brown eyes.

"And that," Freddie pointed to the dark-haired boy wearing glasses, "is Dictionary Boy, Eighth Seat on the Council."

Dictionary Boy looked up from his book.

"Good to meet you, Jon. Do you know in American English, 'john' can mean an informal word for lavatory, and—"

"STOP!" Arabella threw a ball of dough. It hit Dictionary Boy in the side of the head.

"Ouch!" he said, and frowned at her.

Malcolm and Cool T laughed.

"Don't mind *Thesaurus* Boy," Lickety Split said. "He doesn't mean to offend, and Dad and Malcolm laugh at anything."

Dictionary Boy scowled. "Just a piece of information, that's all."

"Enough information," Joy said. "Food's ready."

Everyone grabbed chapattis and served themselves with the curry.

Jon looked across at Cool T′s mug, more like a mixing bowl.

"It is, isn't it?" Cool T raised his mug to Jon. "I *love* my tea."

"Does everyone read minds up here?" Jon said.

Danny Loco burst through the door and ran to the table.

"Working on a new formula, son?" Joy said. "I used to be the same."

Danny Loco nodded and sat next to Lickety Split.

The mixture of coconut, apple, and beef flavours danced on Jon's tongue. The tender meat melted in his mouth.

"Ever tasted anything like it, Jon?" Danny Loco grabbed a chapatti and filled it with curry. "Is Mum a chef, or what?"

Jon nodded, his mouth too full to answer with words.

"She's a great scientist, too, and used to be Fourth Seat on the Council. Great Switcher in her time. Did more switches than anyone. New recruits like Teal could learn a lot from her." He took a bite, and the curry shot out and landed on his shirt.

"Enough," Joy said. "Next you'll be saying I'm responsible for Teal's destiny."

Malcolm spat out a piece of curry. Everyone looked. He rushed from the room.

Max gaped and stared over Teal's shoulder. The hay dropped from his mouth. Teal spun around in the shed and came face to face with her Spirit Guide. The eagle flapped his enormous wings. Teal shuddered.

151

"You haven't remembered a single dream, have you?" he said.

Teal had tried. "I thought you couldn't come down here."

"This is an emergency," he said. "Do NOT get involved in the Joya Crisis."

Teal heard a car door slam and jumped up. She heard Jon's mum drive off. She looked about her, then ran around the shed.

"What are you looking for?" Max said.

"Where did he go?"

"Who?"

Teal ran up all flights of the condo just in case.

"The eagle?" Max said.

"Yes, where did he go?"

"Teal, it's a dream. You've been shouting out *eagle*."

A *dream*? A dream. What did it mean? She shook her head. It didn't mean anything. She'd read the rule book in the Switcher Centre; rule fifty-seven: *In the event of Joya Crisis, first-time Switchers return to Joya.*

Teal's Magi Pod buzzed purple light and brought her out of her thoughts. The Magi Pod read: Transmission in two.

She grabbed the Magi Pod in her mouth and jumped towards the shed door. She used her nail through the gap to lift the latch and fell into the garden.

She ran to the back door of the house, jumped up at the door handle, pulled it down with her paw, and landed on her giant feet. The door stayed shut. She tried again, pushed her weight at the door, and it opened. She had a minute before transmission.

She raced upstairs and jumped on the bed. Zeus woke with a start, and Teal dropped the Magi Pod.

"Transmission," she said, and got her breath back.

Zeus sat up and rubbed his hands over his face. The Magi Pod buzzed purple light.

"Verify," Darcy said.

"Switcher Teal and Switcher Zeus in attendance," Teal said.

"What's the status of your current mission?"

Teal puffed out her chest. "Letter's written and posted."

"Okay, let's hope it works. You both have to leave."

Teal shot a look at Zeus. He raised upturned hands.

"I'll be down to brief you and take you to your new location. I'll bring stand-ins for you both. We have enough upset without Jon and Jen having to cut their stay."

The transmission closed.

Teal looked at Zeus. "What's going on?"

Zeus ran his fingers through his hair. "If it's what I think it is ... nah, can't be."

"What do you think it is?" Teal said.

"They'd send you back. It can't be."

"Zeus, tell me: What do you *think* it is?"

"A Joya Crisis."

Cool T pulled up on his quad bike. Jon's eyes widened.

Captivated by the sight and sound, Jon stepped off the quad and stumbled. He tilted his head back and stared. Ten-metre golden panpipes glistened in the sun and repeated an eight-note melody.

"I'm coming in," Cool T said. "I need to see Hobo."

"Good afternoon," someone said. "Welcome to the Golden Gates of Discovery."

Jon looked either side of him.

"Oy! Down here."

Jon looked down at an orange doormat.

"Stand on me," the mat said.

Jon looked at Cool T, who nodded. Jon put half a foot on the mat.

"Come on, both feet. I don't bite, not on your first day anyway."

Jon laughed and stepped on. Two hands emerged from the mat. They gripped his feet and yanked them beneath the mat. Jon gulped. He couldn't move. His toes tingled then his legs filled with pins and needles. The prickling spiralled up his spine. His face started to go numb.

"STOP!"

The hands pushed his feet back to the surface, then disappeared beneath the mat.

"The first time is the worst," Cool T said. "It needs to get a good reading."

"Gold door," the mat said. "Off you go."

Jon sprang off the mat and rubbed his face with his hands.

The gates opened, and vanilla wafted up his nose. A red snaky path stood in a field abounding with square cream-coloured flowers. The path ended at twenty bronze steps, the risers encrusted in emeralds.

At the top of the steps stood a stone building in the shape of a giant crown, emeralds adorning its peaks. The gold door stood in the centre, other coloured doors wrapped around the crown.

"Go on, then," the mat said.

Jon closed his mouth and walked up the path with Cool T, the panpipes playing behind them.

The gold door opened as they reached the top step. Jon could hear Freddie singing:

"Reiki rocks! Reiki rocks! Lay those healing hands on me. Reiki rocks, Reiki rocks. Give me those healing hands, oh, please, Reiki rocks …"

Jon walked in to find cats, dogs, ferrets, and humans dancing on armchairs.

Hobo turned the stereo off.

"Come on in, just getting the energy flowing before we start. This is Jon the Trader. Let's give him a Freddie welcome."

All the students shouted together, "Reiki rocks! Reiki rocks!"

Jon laughed and sat down next to a tan ferret.

"Portia," she said. "Good to meet you."

"You too," Jon said, then looked to the front of the room.

Hobo frowned at Cool T. "What can I do for *you*?"

"Headache in my eyes. Can you take a look?"

Cool T took off his shades, and Hobo's eyes widened.

"Who's hypnotized you?"

"*What*?"

Hobo placed his hands over Cool T´s eyes.

"Ah, I see. Well, the secret's safe with me."

Jon wished he could read minds. What secret? Who *had* hypnotized Cool T?

Hobo took his hands away.

"Better?" He asked. Cool T nodded but looked worried.

"Better let Darcy know," Hobo said.

Cool T left, and Hobo turned back to the class.

"Okay, guys," Hobo said. "Back to basics today for our guest. Good chance to go over what you know. Portia, what does Reiki mean?"

"Universal energy," the tan ferret said.

"Good. What does it do?" Hobo asked.

A girl in the front put up her hand. "Makes you feel wonderful."

Hobo winked at Jon. "Want to have a Reiki treatment?"

Jon shrugged and nodded. Hobo pulled a bed from the edge of the room.

"You can lie down or sit to receive Reiki."

Jon sat on the bed, then decided to lie down.

"I'm going to place my hands over or directly on your whirling wheels, okay?" Hobo said.

Jon nodded, the scent of vanilla still in his nose.

"We want all those wheels, including the ones above your head, to be spinning, no blockages."

Hobo placed his hands on Jon's crown. Jon felt heat pour through his head. A white light seemed to be cleansing through his body. It made him smile—he couldn't help it.

"Good," Hobo said.

Hobo's hands hovered above Jon's neck without touching him. Jon felt a twinge in his neck and then it seemed as if warm honey had coated his throat.

He drifted off to a sea of ice cream and woke up to feel Hobo's hands on his feet. He felt as if he could float around the room.

"Okay, you're done," Hobo said.

Already?

"It's been over an hour."

"Wow. That's amazing. I feel so calm."

Hobo passed him a water and smiled. "Cleared some of that anger with your dad, that's why."

Jon glanced around the room, but no one else seemed to care except him.

Julius Webb looked out of his lab window and beyond to the park. The grass had been purple for a moment, hadn't it? He blinked and tutted. He dug his fingers into his temples, the pain made him crazy.

Darcy flashed in his mind and he sneered. He wanted her to suffer.

The queen had told her truth, the others would follow. Darcy would come down. She had to. He needed to get on, work through this pain. He had to be ready.

Darcy met Cool T on the black stone path hidden by the trees.

"Darcy, I'm sorry, Julius hypnotized me."

Darcy closed her eyes.

"*I'm* sorry," she said when she opened them. "I shouldn't have sent you. What did you tell him? Do you remember?"

Cool T flinched. "I do now. I told him he might get you down to Earth if he used the royal family."

Darcy nodded. Her Magi Pod buzzed purple light.

"I have to get back to Discovery," Cool T said. "Pick up Jon."

Darcy looked from her Magi Pod to Cool T.

"Who knows?"

"Just Hobo," Cool T said.

"Good. Let's keep it that way."

Jon got back to his den, full of energy. He picked up his Blib. He held it in front of himself.

"Record," he said. The Blib showered him in red crumbs.

"Hi, Teal. I've just been to Discovery. What a place! Cool T said the music in the gates is one of Freddie's songs."

He took a breath.

"Oh, I thought about Zeus punching Pigbreath in boxing. I got rid of the thought as soon as it came, but if Rocket Ron found out …"

He shook his head.

"So don't tell me secret stuff, just to be safe. Blimey, how do you cope with everyone knowing what's inside your head up here?

"How's your assignment going? Brilliant, I bet. The RSPCA letter sounded great. Anyway, my Chief Switcher friend, do me proud. Love, Jon. Send."

Jon blew on the Blib, placed it back in the laptop, and sat down to play PowerSword. The game welcomed him back, and he lost himself in it.

He wanted to go over the boxing. He did some stretches and set the alarm for twenty minutes—any more and he wouldn't have any arms for tomorrow. He pulled on his boxing gloves.

Before he knew it, a song blared from the floor.

"The world of Joya, The world of Joya …"

Jon grinned. He recognized that voice.

The DJ came in over the end of the song.

"Freddie Maya does it again with another knock-out tune, straight in at Number One. This next track is—"

Jon kicked the radio alarm football and it switched off. His dad popped in his mind, but for the first time, anger didn't.

Teal heard Max wake up. *Finally.* She let out a sigh, then ran up to the fourth floor of the condo.

"Max, we're leaving."

"I thought you said six weeks," Max said.

"We're being called off on another mission."

"So are Jon and Jen coming back?" Max said.

"No. You're getting temporary stand-ins, and Darcy's coming down to take us, I know you're not crazy about dogs."

"I'm not crazy about you going either," Max said. "I'll miss you."

A lump wedged in Teal's throat.

"Should be just a few days, then I'll be back."

She closed her eyes. Please let it only be a few days.

Jon woke to knocking on his door. He picked up the football alarm: eight-thirty. The knocking got harder.

He opened the door, and a shocking pink Bulletin Bean flew straight towards him. He ducked just in time. It hit the ceiling, then crashed down to the floor, then jumped up and down, shouting, "Bulletin Bean! Bulletin Bean! Bulletin Bean for Jon the Trader!"

It stopped jumping and sat on the floor.

"Come on, man! Open me up. Places to go, people to see."

Jon picked it up, and the Bulletin Bean opened in his hands. A piece of purple paper flew skyward. Jon jumped and snatched it from midair. He placed the Bulletin Bean back on the floor and read the note.

> Morning Jon,
> If you're up for an early start, I'm ready when you are. Loads to learn. Turn right out of your place, mine's the first door you come to on your left. Can't miss it.
> Danny Loco

The Bulletin Bean spoke. "Close the Bean, I'm outta this scene!"

Jon closed the Bulletin Bean, and it flew out of the den shouting, "I gotta fly, saying bye-bye!"

Jon turned right down the twisty corridor. The first door on the left, a huge steel door, had *Professor Danny Loco's Laboratorial Residence* written in exploding purple gunk. The purple pestle hanging from the door had to be the door knocker. Jon practiced his boxing moves to dodge the exploding gunk. He kept one hand in front of his face, grabbed the metal pestle with the other, and knocked on the steel door. It boomed like a bass drum and opened.

Jon ducked, then ran into the biggest laboratory he had ever seen. Pots bubbled, tubes of different coloured liquids hissed.

"Impressive, huh?" Danny Loco was crushing some golden pips.

Jon nodded. He lifted his purple arms. "Does this come off?" he asked.

"Sometimes."

Jon spat on his fingers and rubbed his arm. He wandered over to a plastic model sitting in a giant hand. The globe at the base had a fuzzy cloud around it and a pole sticking out of it. A small red and purple dish balanced on the end of the pole.

"Is that Earth?"

Danny Loco nodded. "Mmm. First Trader to have noticed." He pointed to the little dish. "Joya follows Earth's orbit, keeping close. The fuzzy cloud you see signifies the atmosphere around Earth, composed of oxygen and nitrogen. With me so far?"

"Yes."

"Earth is the only known planet to support life, and in effect that's literal, because without Earth, Joya wouldn't survive."

"You feed off our nitrogen and oxygen?"

"A little, yes. Not as much as we used to, and not nearly enough to affect the ozone layer or anything like that—you've messed that up yourselves."

Jon shifted on his feet.

"So how's Earth affected by Joya taking some of our natural gases?"

"It isn't," Danny Loco said. "We take one billionth of what one Earthie uses every day for the whole of this planet. It's so miniscule Earth isn't affected at all. Still, we're grateful for the resource—which is why we give back by helping Earthies."

"Why do you need so little nitrogen and oxygen compared to us?" Jon asked.

"Ooh, good question. It all comes down to the wonderful, renewable, natural resource of Maya dust."

"The stuff that goes in Hobo's hot chocolate?" Jon said.

"One and the same."

"So it helps you breathe?" Jon said.

"Yep. I'm working on a formula that will allow us to breathe with just Maya dust and other elements from Joya. Just in case ..."

"In case?" Jon asked.

Danny Loco shuddered. "In case any Earthie severed our connection."

"Why would they do that?"

"Well, look how defensive *you* got. I quote, 'So how is Earth affected?' I heard the worry in your voice. Imagine if a not-so-balanced Earthie politician found out about us. They'll think Joya has a negative affect on your planet, despite any number of tests we can run to prove otherwise."

Danny Loco had a point. And people from Earth would want in on the Maya dust.

"Why don't you help with world peace or stop wars or something?" Jon said.

"We have to play it safe, and we have rules. Our operation has to be as low key as possible, so we won't be discovered. Who are we to interfere in your business, anyway? Some people say we should leave well alone. But we believe in reciprocity, even if one planet isn't aware."

"Reciprocity?" Jon asked.

"A mutual exchange."

"Well, it's not mutual if we don't know about it, is it?" Jon said.

"What would you have us do? Pop down to Earth and make a little statement? 'Hi. We're from another planet. Okay if we have a bit of your nitrogen and oxygen?'"

Jon saw his point. His mum might not understand and she saw both sides to everything. He'd ask her when he got back.

"Afraid not," Danny Loco said.

"You don't trust her?"

"Nothing of the sort," Danny Loco said. "Before you leave, we give you an injection of Missing Memory Potion."

"I hate injections."

"It's okay. A small prick in your thumb. You don't even feel it. You'll remember Joya as a dream that fades over time."

"I don't want to remember it as a dream. It's real, I don't want it to fade." Jon felt his face get hot. He clenched his fists. "And how could I forget a dog on a motorbike dropping me off?"

"As your Maya transporter, Darcy or whoever takes you back flies into the air on their vehicle. Your logical Earth mind deletes the image, because it doesn't fit with what you believe to be true on Earth. It has to be like this, Jon, or we'd be discovered in no time. You can stop the *dreams* from fading by using the Joya learnings on Earth."

"Well, I think it's a shame," Jon said.

"So do we, Jon. So do we."

Chapter 12

Julius Webb laughed like a madman and punched the air. Sharp pain pierced through his skull. He winced. He closed one eye, it helped somehow. He pressed the back of his head against the cold leather sofa. The newscaster repeated the main story.

> The Chancellor of the Exchequer has announced he plans to double taxes because he wants to buy himself an island.

Julius wondered when Joya would hear the news. Had they already linked him with it all? Darcy would have. He eased himself out of the sofa, went back to his lab, and finished the surprise that would terrify her.

Zeus, Teal, and Max all sat in the shed. Rain pummelled the roof. The shed door opened and Darcy walked in. She shook her fur and pelted them all with water.

"Sorry," she said.

"What's the plan, Darcy?" Zeus asked.

"Jon and Jen will stay on Joya. Your temporary fill-ins are outside."

"Have the fill-ins had time to study Jon and Jen?" Teal asked.

"Well, you did, and then didn't act like Jen at all."

Teal hung her head.

"Come on," Darcy said. "You're going to be royals."

Teal shot a glance at Zeus, and saw the shock in *his* eyes too.

Darcy introduced Zeus and Teal to Prince George. Teal wondered if she should say something about her dreams. This had gone way out of her comfort zone. Last night, in a dream, she had seen her dad crying in the cave.

"Prince George has arranged to see his grandmother tomorrow," Darcy said. "See if there's a connection between the corgi and what the queen said."

"I take it I'll have to go alone," Zeus said.

Teal let out a breath and relaxed her shoulders.

"No," Darcy said. "You both go."

Teal frowned and Darcy placed a paw on her shoulder.

"Teal, I'm counting on you, with those great instincts of yours, to find anything unusual."

Teal forced a smile, nodded, and pushed the dreams to the back of her mind.

Darcy handed Prince George a dart. He left the room and returned with his black rabbit in his arms.

"This is Polo," Darcy said. "At least he has smaller feet."

Teal looked but said nothing.

Darcy and Zeus bombarded the prince with questions about mannerisms, habits, and how he addressed the queen.

Darcy wished her Switchers good luck, and before Teal could scream, *Take me back!* Darcy had flown off with Prince George and Polo.

Hi Brid, Darcy and Malcolm had a meeting in the Assembly Room.

"I think I've met Teal's Spirit Guide," Malcolm said.

Hi Brid raised his eyes. "Think?"

"Well, he didn't speak. It's an eagle."

"I don't think *Teal* would have an eagle. How do you know, if it didn't speak?"

"I just felt it."

"Right. Whatever."

Darcy wondered.

"Where's the prince, Darcy?" Hi Brid said.

"In Zeus's quarters. No one will go there while Zeus is away."

"So is he allowed out?" Malcolm said.

"Of course. He isn't a prisoner. We just don't want to have to explain things to you know who if we don't have to."

"So what do we know for sure?" Malcolm said.

"That the queen's not herself, that she received a corgi from Julius Webb, and that the same day she announced she never wanted to be queen."

"It could all be coincidence," Hi Brid said.

Malcolm nodded. "After all, how could he know anything? Arabella gave him the potion."

Darcy shook her head. "How do we know he took it? If he didn't drink it all, the memory would come back. I should have checked."

"You think he'd wait sixteen years for revenge?" Malcolm said.

"We don't know when—or how much—memory came back. Assuming it did. At this moment in time, I don't know *what* to think."

The Magi Screen buzzed purple light. They all turned.

"Switcher Teal with urgent transmission."

Darcy felt a hand grab her insides. "Go ahead, Switcher."

"The chancellor's just said on TV he's going to buy an island with taxpayers´ money."

Hi Brid closed his eyes. Malcolm bit his lip.

171

"Anything else?" Darcy asked.

"His pet parrot said some other things. None of them as bad as the island. Do you want me to list them?"

Darcy closed her eyes. "No."

"Daily learnings?" Teal said.

"Forget them," Darcy said. "Find out what you can with the queen today and report back. Closing transmission."

"Now what?" Hi Brid asked.

"Emergency switch," Darcy said. "I'll get Cool T to download all information on the chancellor."

Hi Brid nodded. "Malcolm, you'll switch with the chancellor. Freddie can be the parrot. Go find him. Tell him everything."

The chancellor paced 11 Downing Street, shaking his head. How could he have told the nation about his island? He held his hand over his mouth—he couldn't trust what would come out next. He didn't answer the door or phone. He looked at the parrot. She repeated every truth he uttered, like the conscience he'd never had.

Julius pushed the safety pin into the fire extinguisher. He had filled it with carbon dioxide, methanol, and other substances that destroy nitrogen and oxygen on impact. With the force from the extinguisher he could blast straight through the connection, and Darcy would give him the coordinates. He wouldn't use it, of course, but *she* didn't know that. Oh, he'd scare her, all right.

Jon and Danny Loco went off to the kitchen for a late lunch. Jon's mind felt like Danny's door—exploding with information.

Freddie sat at the big table.

"Hey, guys," he said. "You're eating late."

"We've been learning," Danny Loco said. "What's your excuse?"

Freddie jumped down from the stool. "Got summoned. Busy."

"Are you okay?" Jon said.

"Gotta fly." Freddie ran out of the kitchen.

"What's that about?"

"Don't know," Danny Loco said. "But he's masking his thoughts."

Jon frowned. He had to learn how to read them. Maybe Teal knew how. She could help him.

Danny Loco went over to the hob.

"Has your mum cooked today?" Jon said.

"Nope. This isn't her chilli. Is *your* mum a good cook?" Danny Loco brought the chilli over to the table.

"She's terrible." Jon lowered his head. "My dad used to cook."

"Used to?"

"He left. A year ago."

"Been on sandwiches ever since?" Danny Loco said.

Jon didn't laugh.

"Hey, come on, man. At least you had a dad for a while. Mine? Dead. Never even got to meet him. I've got Hi Brid, I guess. He's sort of always been around supporting me, but. . ."

"Sorry. I'm just mad at him," Jon said.

"Yeah, Hi Brid makes me mad sometimes."

"Not Hi Brid! My dad, for leaving."

"That why you don't play football anymore?"

"Do you know everything?"

"Pretty much. What's to gain by not playing?"

"If he knew I'd stopped maybe he'd come back. One player got dropped by the new coach, I've become his human football."

"Ah, Pigbreath," Danny Loco said.

"Blimey, you do know everything."

Danny Loco nodded. "You're not the reason your dad went. He is."

"What?"

"You're angry, but here's the thing. Parents are just people with a title. They mess up. He left *you*. It's his loss, mate."

The chilli fell off Jon's spoon. The realization set in. He needed to move on.

Jon slept for a few hours and woke to a rap at the door. He opened it and ducked.

Cool T laughed, giant mug in hand. "Expecting a Bulletin Bean?"

"Last one nearly took my head off," Jon said.

Cool T nodded. "Yeah, I need to reprogram them to be less in your face. Pardon the pun."

"You designed them?" Jon said.

"I'm the castle techie."

"Wow. Do they think for themselves?"

"No. It's a computer program, reacts after certain time delays, so people read the messages and give the beans back. They try and keep the gold ones."

"I haven't had a gold one."

"They're given out by Hi Brid to acknowledge special achievements. They're called Brilliant Beans, but most of us call them Gold Beans. If you get one, there's a big celebration. Hi Brid doesn't send many."

"Have you ever gotten one?" Jon asked.

"Enough with the questions. I'm hungry. I came to say I'm off to the kitchen to grab some dinner. You coming?"

Jon nodded.

"For the third time, I'm charged and holding a message."

Jon spun round to see his Blib in the laptop bursting with orange. He beamed.

"Must have been a deep sleep," Cool T said. "The second reminder is pretty loud."

Jon bit his lip and looked from the Blib to Cool T.

"No problem. Stay here," Cool T said. "Want me to send a sandwich down?"

"Thanks," Jon said.

He shut the door and ran over to the Blib.

He blew on it twice, directed it at the wall, and Teal appeared in front of him. He grinned.

"Hi, Jon," she said. "Glad you like Discovery. Yes, you're right, better we don't say anything that could be read in your thoughts. Lucky escape with Rocket Ron, well done."

She raised her forepaw and bit on a nail.

"I've got something on my mind, I could do with running it past you. . ." She sighed and shook her head.

"It's not worth the risk. By the way, loads of Mayas can't read thoughts, we're just unlucky you're surrounded by the ones that can. It's a pain."

She shook her head.

"Sorry, I sound like a right misery. I'll send you an upbeat Blib tomorrow, I promise. G´nite. Loads of love, your friend Teal."

Jon ran his hand through his hair. He wished he hadn't told her about the gym. She needed to speak to him. He wanted to help her, but if she told him something how could he promise to hide his thoughts?

He played the message again. She didn't smile once.

PC Frank Willis sat in front of the television and rubbed his forehead.

His mum placed her hands on her hips. "Did you have anything to do with this, Frank?"

"Don't be stupid." He didn't mean to snap.

His mum stormed off to bed. Frank continued watching the late news.

And the top story again. The Chancellor of the Exchequer has announced he is going to buy a tropical island with extra income tax.

They switched to the chancellor's announcement. The parrot landed on the chancellor's shoulder. "Buy me an island! Buy me an island!" it said.

Frank turned the television off and sat there in the dark. First the queen, now this. *Did* he have something to do with it? He'd delivered the pets, nothing more. Something nagged at his brain. The pieces flew around. The box of money, Julius going on the around-the-world trip . . . A haze kept the pieces from joining.

Exhausted from fighting with his thoughts, he dozed off.

He woke up to knocking at the door. He looked at the clock: five a.m. He jumped up to answer it before it woke his mum.

The chief of police stood on the doorstep with a tall, handsome, tanned man in a business suit. He looked like an American quarterback.

"Chief?" Frank rubbed his eyes.

"Yes, Frank. Ten points," the chief said. "*This* is CIA Agent Shatner. He has some questions to ask you. Do you want to do this here or at the station? I presume you don't want your mother involved."

Frank heard a cough behind him. He looked over his shoulder and saw his mother sitting on the stairs in her dressing gown. She looked at him, waiting for an explanation. He wanted to cry.

"Something's come up at the station, Mum." He rushed out the door before she could question him. The three of them drove to the station in silence.

When they arrived, Shatner pushed Frank in one of the interview rooms and locked the door.

Jon had a fretful night of dreams in which Teal was in danger. He woke in a sweat and ran to his Blib: Empty. He showered and got dressed, the dreams still vivid in his mind.

He met Danny Loco outside the castle. They flew to boxing on his rocket.

Jon partnered Lickety Split, Dictionary Boy partnered Danny Loco, and Cool T partnered Rocket Ron Johnson.

They began with sit-ups, press-ups, and skipping, then put on gloves and pads.

"I want to demonstrate a right hook for Jon." Rocket Ron pulled on his gloves. "Dictionary Boy, come hold the pads."

Dictionary Boy walked over at a snail's pace. Jon couldn't blame him. Who would want Rocket Ron hitting him?

"So the pad is at the side." Rocket Ron placed Dictionary Boy's pad in the right place. "You need to twist your hips as you come round, and hit that pad." Rocket Ron thundered a hook that could have blown a hole through the pad. Dictionary Boy grimaced and Rocket Ron demonstrated again and again.

"Dictionary Boy," Rocket Ron said. "Your reflexes are lightning fast but your strength stinks." He shook his head. "If you came more often …" He sighed and looked around at the rest of the class. "Now, to get more power in those shots, you twist back more before you swing around, like this."

Dictionary Boy struggled to keep his feet on the floor.

"Okay, all of you, let's see how it's done."

Jon twisted back and threw the hook. He shocked himself at the power. He didn't use his dad any more, just pure adrenaline—and he loved it.

"See what you can do without him?" Rocket Ron said. "Nice power."

Jon beamed and did more right and left hooks until his shoulders burned. He swapped to pads so Lickety Split could practice.

"Okay, enough for today," Rocket Ron said.

Jon left the gym with the others. They all arranged to meet up at the park for a Hobo special. They had earned it.

Hobo laughed when he saw them.

"Nice to see you tomatoes!"

"Good workout, Hobo," Cool T said.

"Yeah, well," Hobo said. "We all know 'good workout' to you means 'almost a killer' to the rest of us." Hobo poured them all a Choco Works.

They talked to him until more customers came up, then moved over to the Funky Fountain.

"You've got a fast jab, Jon," Cool T said. "Rocket Ron praised you up, too, and that doesn't happen."

"Thanks. I love it. I never thought about boxing training before, now I'm addicted. I've even woken myself up punching the air in my sleep."

"Been there." Danny Loco wiped the chocolate off his nose. "Your skill's stepped up a gear without the anger, huh?"

Jon nodded and grinned at his friend. His thoughts wandered to another friend. Why hadn't Teal sent him a message?

Chapter 13

Zeus ended his call to the queen. He sat back in the sofa and ran his hands through his hair.

"What did she say, Zeus?" Teal said.

"She's postponed us till seven."

Teal closed her eyes.

"I don't think I'm up to this. What if I can't tell what's unusual? What if I'm not experienced enough to spot anything."

"Have faith in yourself, Teal. I do, so does Darcy."

She ran her paw over the Blib. She hadn't sent Jon another message. She couldn't trust herself to hide her fear and didn't want him to worry.

"Stop padding the carpet, come and watch some TV," Zeus said.

Teal jumped up next to him on the sofa. They watched a chat show before the news. It seemed to be a shocker of a week for headlines:

The prime minister has made a public confession of an unusual nature. It would appear he has a shoe fetish.

The camera switched to a press conference. The prime minister, a middle-aged man so ordinary-looking you'd be hard put to describe him five minutes after meeting him, stood in front of a podium.

I would like the nation to know that in my spare time I wear women's shoes.

He proceeded to answer questions from journalists about favourite types, colours, and heel height. "Of course," he said, "I'm lucky to have small feet."

Teal looked at Zeus. "I guess this is abnormal."

"Just a bit," Zeus said. "Better let Darcy know."

The prime minister's wife screamed at him.

"Why did you say it? Are you crazy? We've kept it secret for years." She threw some sweaters into the suitcase. "*WHY?*"

The prime minister sat on the bed. He'd persuaded his wife to get away from the media until things died down.

He had no idea why and fought with the urge to tell her how the skirt she had on, the one she thought he liked, made her stomach look like a pouch with a little joey sleeping inside.

"What?" she asked.

"It looks like a baby kang ..." he put his hand over his mouth.

"*What?*"

He rushed out of the room and locked himself in the bathroom before he could do any more damage.

Darcy walked into the Assembly Room. Hi Brid sat on a green cushion.

"You wanted to see me?" Darcy said.

Hi Brid rubbed his forehead. "What's Prince George up to?"

"Virtual fishing in Zeus's den. Hobo's dropped off a Choco Works, so he's happy."

"What about his rabbit?"

"She's with Jen at the Open Circus, she's fine. I could've told you this via Magi Pod. What's going on?"

"Teal," Hi Brid said. "We need to get her back here."

"I agree. Rule fifty-seven."

"Darcy …" He ran his fingers through his hair and pulled his head back.

She waited. Her fur bristled.

"The eagle, her Spirit Guide, came to me ten minutes ago."

"And?"

Hi Brid looked at her, put a hand on her shoulder.

"*What?*"

"He's seen her last breath on Earth."

Darcy's eyes widened.

The Magi Screen buzzed purple light.

"Switcher Teal with news item."

"Proceed," Hi Brid said.

"Prime minister has announced he wears women's shoes."

Hi Brid sighed. "Is this a joke?"

"No. He has a shoe fetish."

Darcy and Hi Brid looked at each other. Darcy turned to the Magi Pod.

"When is your meeting with the queen?"

"Twenty minutes."

No time to switch them back.

"Okay. Find out something, anything, from your meeting with the queen. Afterwards, you and Zeus come back."

Darcy closed the connection.

PC Frank Willis had been alone in the interview room for hours. The door opened and Agent Shatner walked in. What did the CIA have to do with all of this?

Agent Shatner sat down, put a bag on the floor, and crossed his giant hands on the table.

"Your record up to now has been impeccable, Frank. Why did you do this?"

"Do what?" Frank said.

Agent Shatner glared, Frank shrank back.

"I've got jet lag, and believe me, I don't need your wisecracks on top."

Frank bit his nails. "I don't know what I've done."

"I'd like to believe you, Frank. I don't like what other prisoners do to police officers in prison."

A shiver ran through Frank's spine.

"I don't understand what I'm here for," Frank said.

"We know you took a bribe and I think I know from who."

The box of money.

"Now tell me everything from the moment you met Julius Webb. I want every detail." Agent Shatner leaned back in his chair and locked his hands behind his head.

Frank told him.

Agent Shatner sat for some moments, staring. Frank's sweat rolled down his forehead and soaked through his shirt.

Shatner reached in the bag and pulled out a wad of money. "Spent any?"

Frank felt sick. "You've searched my house? My mum ..."

"Only your house. We didn't search your mom." Agent Shatner laughed, then shook his head and got up from his chair. "Greener than a class-A booger."

Frank put his head in his hands.

Zeus and Teal waited in a room full of antique furniture in Buckingham Palace. Zeus sat in a red and gold high-backed chair. Teal paced the floor in front of him.

"How exciting, Teal," Zeus said. "We're going to meet the queen."

"Exciting for you, maybe." Teal turned towards Zeus. She hadn't listened to her dad. Or her Spirit Guide.

"What's wrong?" Zeus said.

"I had a dream."

"And?"

"I guess I can tell you now, we're going back anyway."

Zeus sat on the edge of the seat. "You've got me intrigued."

Teal took a deep breath. "My Spirit Guide came to me in a dream, warned me not to—"

The queen entered with her corgi.

"Oh, you've brought your rabbit," she said. "That's silly, with dogs all around the palace."

Zeus shot a glance at Teal, snatched her up into his arms and squashed the breath out of her.

"I didn't think," he said.

"Quite." The queen raised her eyes. "Sorry, George. Can't seem to stop this darn directness. No offence, you understand."

"None taken." Zeus released his grip on Teal and reached for his cup and saucer. "How's the new corgi?"

"Poor little Lancelot. He's nervous, I don't know why. He nipped me when he first met me."

"Grandmother," Zeus said. "You didn't tell me."

"Well, it's a little scratch and Lancelot had such a sad face afterwards." She smiled at the dog. "No harm done."

The bite. Teal tried to get Zeus's attention. She put her forepaws on Zeus's stomach and head-butted the saucer. He pushed her back down into his lap and stroked her head, his eyes on the queen.

Teal saw the corgi's eyes—they looked like Darcy's at the Open Circus when Hobo had hypnotized her. Oh my gosh, that's *it*. The dog has been hypnotized and it bit the queen. Teal had to get Zeus out of there and tell him.

But Zeus wouldn't look down at her, and he was drinking his tea at slug speed. When he placed the empty cup and saucer on a side table, Teal took her chance. She couldn't sit still any longer. She jumped off Zeus's lap and thudded to the floor.

Lancelot bared his teeth at Teal, who realised too late that being hypnotized didn't affect the dog's instinctive dislike for rabbits. Lancelot leapt in her direction.

"Lancelot, no!" the queen shouted.

Teal bolted for the small opening in the door. She heard a cup and saucer smash, then felt Lancelot's teeth sink into her rump.

Chapter 14

Darcy picked the lock at the back of 11 Downing Street. Malcolm and Freddie followed her inside. They could hear the parrot:

"Buy me an island! Buy me an island!"

They followed the noise of the bird and pushed a door open. The chancellor, taking up three quarters of a sofa, looked up and screamed. The parrot slipped off its perch.

Darcy had no time for theatrics. She threw a dart at the chancellor, and he slumped forward.

Malcolm laughed. "I thought the parrot got the dart."

"She doesn't need it, she's fainted."

Malcolm took the parrot out of the cage and placed it in his lap. Freddie ran up the sofa next to his friend. He frowned.

"I ain't keen on being a parrot, man."

Darcy bared her teeth at him.

"Just saying, that's all."

Malcolm shook his head, his eyes fixed on the chancellor.

"Just as well you lent Cool T's quad. You'd never persuade him—or squeeze him—onto your bike."

"I'm not waiting," Darcy said.

"What do you mean?" Malcolm said.

"I'm taking them back to Joya while they're *both* unconscious. I'll explain to them there."

Malcolm and Freddie looked from the chancellor to each other. Darcy raised a paw.

"Yes, I know," she said. "I'm breaking Maya law."

"Stuff the law," Freddie said. "How're you gonna move him?"

Darcy nodded twice and transformed into another Malcolm.

"If two Malcolms can't lift him, no one can," she said.

Malcolm eyed Darcy like a mirror and stuck out his chest. "Do I look that good?"

Darcy smiled. "Come on, Freddie, grab the bird."

Freddie took the parrot in his teeth and forepaws. Darcy and Malcolm hauled the chancellor out of the sofa and half-carried, half-dragged him outside. They heaved him onto the quad, and he slumped forward. Malcolm took the parrot from Freddie and worked it into the chancellor's suit pocket.

Darcy nodded, winced, and shrank back down to herself. She shook out her coat and looked at the quad. She didn't like it, but she had no choice.

"Lift him up, Malcolm."

Malcolm pulled the great man up into a sitting position and held him there. Darcy ran up, sat in the chancellor's lap, and grabbed the handlebars.

"Okay, let him go," she said.

His body thumped into hers and pushed the air out of her. She fought to stay upright.

"Is that safe?" Malcolm asked.

"Not really, so I won't hang around." Darcy struggled to speak. "Find out what you can. Good luck." She managed a tight smile and flew off into the sky.

"Lancelot! No!" the queen said.

Zeus had jumped up and knocked the side table, sending his cup and saucer crashing to the floor. Lancelot sank his teeth into Teal. Zeus dived across the floor. He grabbed the corgi by the tail, pulled it off Teal, and threw him across the room. He heard the queen rush over to her dog.

Zeus saw the blood on Teal's rump.

"Teal, are you okay?" he asked.

She didn't move. He looked at her face. Her eyelids drooped, then she closed her eyes. Zeus's heart quickened.

"Grandmother, I need to get her checked out."

She frowned at Zeus and petted Lancelot. "Of course," she said.

Zeus gathered Teal into his arms, her body limp over his limbs. A lump wedged in his throat. He needed a vet. He had to get back to Prince George's and find the number.

Teal mumbled as he placed her on the sofa. "Zeus." Zeus's heart leapt.

"Shhh. Let me get you some help." He reached for the phone.

"Important," Teal said. "It's the bite. Dog's been hypnotized. The eyes."

Zeus opened his mouth to speak, but Teal's eyes closed.

He looked up the emergency vet number in Prince George's mobile. The vet arrived ten minutes later.

When the vet left, Zeus felt as if she'd taken his insides and slammed them in the door. A tear rolled down his cheek.

Darcy landed in front of the Maya Castle. The chancellor stirred and sat up.

"Where am I?"

Darcy jumped down from the quad. She pushed back on her hind legs and stretched out her back.

"Come on."

He heaved himself from the quad and teetered along beside her. As they entered the Assembly Room the parrot emerged from the chancellor's pocket and perched on his shoulder.

"So, please," Hi Brid said. "Leave me to tell Danny."

"*Some* secret!" Lickety Split said. Cool T and Dictionary Boy nodded.

They all looked up.

The chancellor blinked. "Who are you all? Is this a dream?"

Hi Brid raised his eyebrows at Darcy.

The parrot flew across the Assembly Room.

The chancellor called after it. "Come back, Thingy!"

"What sort of name is that?" Lickety Split said.

"She's a present. I haven't had her long."

The members of the Council looked at each other.

"Who gave you the present?" Hi Brid said.

"Julius Webb."

Hi Brid and Darcy closed their eyes.

"Has anyone *else* received a pet?" Hi Brid asked.

"The prime minister, a poodle."

"Dictionary Boy, you're switching with the prime minister," Hi Brid said. "Lickety Split, you'll be the poodle. You've one hour. Go!"

They ran from the Assembly Room.

The Magi Screen buzzed purple light.

"Zeus, is that you?" Darcy said.

"Yes. The queen's been bitten by the corgi. A scratch, that's all." He sounded like he had a cold.

Hi Brid let out a groan. Zeus continued.

"Teal noticed the corgi's been hypnotized. Maybe it's carrying some truth drug."

Hi Brid nodded. "Well *done*, Teal."

"She's unconscious," Zeus said.

"*What?*" Darcy said.

"The corgi bit Teal, she's in a coma. The vet's said she can't be moved. I . . . we don't know how long she's got." Zeus broke down.

Hi Brid and Darcy looked at each other.

"You took this long to tell us?" Hi Brid said.

Darcy gulped. She couldn't speak.

"I should've been firm," Hi Brid said. "What the heck is a rookie doing on Earth in the middle of a Joya Crisis? Do we never learn? Tell us Teal's symptoms."

A sniff came down the Magi Pod.

"NOW!" Hi Brid said.

They couldn't understand Zeus through the tears.

"Zeus," Hi Brid said, "send the symptoms direct to Danny Loco."

195

Darcy shook out her fur, turned to the chancellor. "Did the parrot bite you?"

"Mmhm." He pouted like a child, his eyes glazed.

"Cool T, take the parrot and the chancellor to Danny for blood tests." Hi Brid looked at the chancellor. "When he comes around, you're going to have to explain why he's here."

Cool T raised his eyebrows.

"GO!"

Darcy watched them leave, then turned back to Hi Brid.

"So everyone knows about—"

"Everyone but Danny."

"When are you going to tell him?" Darcy said.

"After the blood tests. Who knows how he'll react. We need his expertise."

"You're like a father to him, Hi Brid."

Hi Brid buried his face in his hands. "Does a father keep something like this from his son?"

Jon sat at the silver table in his den. He stared at the empty Blib. Why hadn't Teal answered his messages? And why had Freddie run off in the kitchen? His mind went back to that night at Hobo's—too late for who? For Teal? Please, don't let it be Teal.

Danny Loco took blood samples from the parrot and the chancellor. The chancellor, resting on a reclining chair with the parrot on his lap, jumped as the metal pestle pounded against the laboratory door. Danny Loco clapped his hands, and the door opened.

Hobo walked in. He wiped purple gunk from his face.

"Hi Brid buzzed me," he said. "The parrot may've been hypnotized."

"What's going on, Hobo?"

"Don't ask me, I'm the last to know. *You're* on the Council."

"Yeah, right. Cool T shielded his thoughts too when he dropped these two off."

Hobo looked at the parrot. "Hypnotized, definitely."

"Who by?" Danny Loco said.

The chancellor sighed. "A friend of mine—Julius Webb."

Hobo looked from the chancellor to Danny Loco, then set to work on the parrot.

Danny Loco listened as the parrot confirmed the chancellor's suspicions: Julius Webb had told three of them to bite their owners and then injected them with something.

"Some friend," Danny Loco said.

His Magi Pod buzzed purple light. He read the text and his mouth fell open.

"What?" Hobo said.

"A message from Zeus: *Danny, help Teal, please. She's dying. The symptoms are ...*"

He looked up. Hobo buried his head in his hands.

Malcolm hung up the phone. He looked around the oak kitchen in 11 Downing Street.

"Well?" Freddie said, flying around above him.

"He's on his way over. Let's hope he doesn't trip in his high heels." Malcolm walked on tiptoes, no mean feat in the chancellor's body.

Freddie shook his head.

"What's wrong?" Malcolm asked.

"I don't like this. I don't like this," Freddie said.

Dictionary Boy and Lickety Split walked in.

"Hey guys. Hey guys," Freddie said.

"Bit of parrot speak get through in the Switch?" Lickety Split said.

"You'll be a poodle soon enough," Freddie said. He kept his beak shut so he couldn't repeat himself.

Lickety Split groaned.

The prime minister arrived with his poodle. Malcolm opened the door with Freddie on his shoulder. The poodle barked at Freddie.

Malcolm led them through to the drawing room. The prime minister looked at the boy with glasses and the girl with plaits, and looked to Chancellor Malcolm for an explanation.

"This is Dictionary Boy and Lickety Split."

They both nodded.

"I'm not the chancellor," Malcolm said. "We already have him, and Prince George."

The prime minister fell into a chair.

"Terrorists," he whispered.

"Do we look like terrorists?"

"What do you want?" the prime minister asked.

Malcolm explained about the gifts from Julius. He looked at the white poodle leaning against the prime minister's leg.

"Has your poodle bitten you?"

"Yes."

"We need to get you to Joya to run tests. You may be in danger."

"I don't want to go anywhere with you."

"You won't be much use here if you're dead," Dictionary Boy said.

The prime minister's face turned grey.

Malcolm shook his head. "Nice one."

"What?" Dictionary Boy said.

"Look, Prime Minister," Malcolm said, "your planet may be in danger, and so is ours."

"Your *planet*?" The prime minister rubbed his forehead.

Malcolm told him about Joya. The prime minister asked a mountain of questions.

"I'm not sure," he said.

"Do you want the queen's dead body on your conscience?" Dictionary Boy said.

The prime minister agreed to switch.

Malcolm gave the poodle a dart. She fell asleep in the prime minister's arms. Dictionary Boy took them outside.

"Finally," Cool T said. Dictionary Boy made the introductions, and Cool T started up his quad.

Hi Brid and Darcy sat on lime-green cushions in the Assembly Room. They stopped mid-conversation when Danny Loco and Hobo walked in.

"Julius Webb hypnotized all three pets," Hobo said. "Told them to bite their new owners. And injected them with something."

"There's another problem," Danny Loco said.

Hi Brid pulled his head back by the hair. "What?"

"The chancellor's collapsed. Mum's taken him to the hospital, and ..."

"And *what?*" Hi Brid said, covering his thoughts.

Danny Loco continued.

"We can't find anything in the blood of the chancellor, or the parrot. We can't confirm the bite caused the truth telling or the collapse."

"Did you get Teal's symptoms?" Hi Brid said.

Danny Loco nodded. "It's beyond me. I don't know where to start."

"I expect more from you. Run every test until you *do* find something."

"What's going on, Hi Brid?" Danny Loco said.

"Teal's in a coma and the chancellor's collapsed. And you have no idea how to save them. Isn't that enough? Go."

Danny Loco stomped out of the Assembly Room.

Chapter 15

Malcolm, as The Chancellor of the Exchequer, stood in front of the microphone at the press conference:

"I resign from government and apologize to the nation. There is no island—a poor joke on my part."

The press screamed questions at him, but he answered none of them.

Dictionary Boy, now the prime minister, took the stage.

"I am shocked at this revelation and can assure the country there will be no tax increase."

"Aren't you embarrassed you wear women's shoes, Prime Minister?" a short male journalist asked.

The other journalists laughed.

Dictionary Boy smiled and waited for the laughter to die down.

"I look after the country with my head and my heart, NOT my shoes."

He raised his hand to stop further questions, then left the press room. The journalists nodded their heads, impressed despite themselves.

Julius Webb sat down to watch the news.

The Chancellor of the Exchequer has resigned. He has made a formal apology. The prime minister has assured the nation that income tax will not be raised. We are joined in the studio by—

Julius switched off the television.

"Fall into my trap, little flies." He chuckled and splattered tea across the room. No one could fight that truth serum. Mayas had switched with the ministers. He laughed out loud.

They always came in twos—which meant, he guessed, at least six of them would be on Earth already. Darcy would come sniffing around his place, and he would be waiting.

Danny Loco ran more tests in his lab. Joy had returned from the hospital to help. He searched her mind; she knew nothing. He didn't expect her to, but why hadn't they told *him*? Why hadn't there been a full Council meeting?

He added a wrong potion to a test tube and it exploded in his hand. Soot covered his face. Joy and Hobo looked but said nothing.

Cool T arrived with the prime minister and his poodle, then left in too much of a hurry.

Hobo de-hypnotized the poodle, her story identical with the parrot's.

They took blood samples and ran some tests. Joy spotted an irregularity in all four, like a virus.

Danny Loco went to the Assembly Room to give the news and get some answers.

The Assembly Room Magi Screen buzzed purple light.

Hi Brid sank down onto a cushion. Darcy paced.

Dictionary Boy's voice came through the screen. "Opening transmission to the Maya Council."

"Proceed," Hi Brid said.

"Announcements to press are done. They've been received as well as can be expected."

"Dictionary Boy made a corking statement," Malcolm said. "Want to hear it?"

"No," Hi Brid said. "Are Freddie and Lickety Split with you?"

"Yes."

"The corgi's bitten the queen," Hi Brid said. "Luckily, she doesn't have any side effects."

"That's great new—"

"The corgi's also bitten Teal … she's in a coma. She is *not* expected to survive."

Silence.

"The chancellor's also critical. Danny Loco's working on an antidote. I want two of you at Julius's house now—see if *he* has an antidote. Be warned. If he's there, he'll be waiting."

Hi Brid closed the connection.

All four switchers at 10 Downing Street looked at each other.

"We've never lost a Switcher," Dictionary Boy said.

Malcolm brought a hand to his head. "I think I need to lie down, I feel dizzy."

"You okay? You okay?" Freddie tutted with his beak.

"I'll go with Dictionary Boy, check out Julius's place," Lickety Split said. "I can change colour, and the prime minister can pass for anyone."

Freddie nodded.

The prime minister blended into the crowd, although to be safe Dictionary Boy put on a wig—surprised to find quite a few among a range of stilettos in the prime minister's wardrobe.

Lickety Split blinked. Her white fur changed to black.

Dictionary Boy rang a discreet taxi service and arranged to meet the taxi away from Number 10. He slipped out the emergency exit with Lickety Split.

The taxi driver pulled up in the next road to Julius's. Dictionary Boy asked the taxi driver to wait, promising an insane amount of money.

They approached Julius's house and hid behind some hedges. The house looked empty: no lights on, no car on the drive.

"Urghh," Lickety Split said.

Dictionary Boy looked at her. "What?"

"I hate coming down here as a dog," she said. "You know how I love to lick things? Well, I keep getting a desire to lick my own bum. I'll throw up if I do, I tell you. Licking the paws is bad enough."

Dictionary Boy chuckled. "Least you're a poodle."

"Meaning?" Lickety Split asked.

"Poodles don't moult. At least you won't get fur in your mouth."

"What don't you know?" she said.

Dictionary Boy beamed.

"Doesn't look like he's in," she said. "Shall we go for it?"

He nodded.

They ran across the lawn to the front door. Dictionary Boy took a piece of wire from his pocket and picked the lock.

"You think a prime minister does this?" he said.

He opened the door, walked in, and looked over his shoulder at Lickety Split.

"What's wrong?" she said.

"Someone's here."

Lickety Split followed him in and pushed the door closed behind her. "I can smell peppermint." She went to the mug on the coffee table and touched it with her paw.

"It's warm."

"Look out!" Dictionary Boy said.

Julius sprang out from behind a sofa and whacked Lickety Split across the head with a saucepan. She lay on her side, tongue out.

Julius dived across the coffee table. Dictionary Boy jumped, fell backward over the beanbag, and his legs flew in the air. He landed on his back. Julius grabbed his ankle and kicked the beanbag out of the way. Dictionary Boy looked to the front door and thrashed about to free his ankle.

Julius tightened his grip and grabbed the other leg. He pushed them to the ground, then plonked down on Dictionary Boy's thighs.

Dictionary Boy yelped, then gaped at Julius.

You're—"

A fist flew towards Dictionary Boy's face. He grabbed Julius's arm midair and clamped his teeth down into his flesh. His teeth pierced the skin; he tasted blood in his mouth.

Julius screamed and rolled off Dictionary Boy's legs. Dictionary Boy spat out a bit of blood and threw a left uppercut to Julius's chin. His hand met solid rock. The pain shot down Dictionary Boy's arm.

He jumped up. His legs tingled. He threw himself at the window and smashed straight through it. He crashed to the ground, landed on his right knee, and forced himself up. Without looking over his shoulder, he shot back to the taxi, his legs full of pins and needles, his knee screaming.

The taxi driver looked at the blood on his face. Dictionary Boy handed him a wad of notes. The taxi driver opened his mouth and closed it.

"Drive," Dictionary Boy said.

Agent Shatner saw a man fly through the window and run down the street. What the—? He glanced over his shoulder, then up to the house. He sat back. He'd move when Julius moved. But before he knew it, he had dozed off.

"Jon, open up. It's Hobo."

Hobo? Jon walked across the den and opened the door.

"Hi. No Discovery today," Hobo said. "You've got an afternoon in the park."

Jon looked round at the empty Blib in the laptop.

"I'll treat you to a Choco Works," Hobo said. "You'll get to fly on my Harley."

Why hadn't Teal sent him a message?

"I'd rather stay here, Hobo, if that's okay."

"Come on. I'll have customers screaming at me otherwise."

Jon bit the inside of his cheek and looked back at the Blib.

Hobo sighed. "Okay, bring the laptop with you, and a game or two."

Danny Loco strode into the Assembly Room. Cool T looked up from the Joya Crisis handbook.

Hi Brid shifted on a lime-green cushion. Darcy paced and shook her head. She cared about her Switchers. Danny admired that about her.

"Hi Brid. I can't wait any more," Darcy said. "Teal's dying. I'm going to her."

"We're being set up." Hi Brid said.

"I know." She glanced at Danny Loco. "That's why, no matter what, you three *must* stay here. If something happens, we still have the basis for a new Council."

She ran out.

"What's going on, Hi Brid?" Danny Loco said.

"I don't know where to start," Hi Brid said.

"The beginning?"

Hi Brid rubbed his hand over his mouth and looked at Cool T. Cool T shot his eyes down into the book.

"Your mother, as you know, is an ex-Switcher," Hi Brid said. "One of the best, and a valuable member of the Council in her time." He sighed. "She went to Earth a *lot*. She always applied for extra switches and we always obliged her because, well, she did a great job. We should've been more aware."

"Of what?"

"Your mother met and fell in love with an Earthie."

Danny Loco dropped onto a cushion. The ultimate taboo. The worst crime.

Hi Brid continued.

"When she didn't have assignments on Earth, she snuck him back here in her rocket."

"And you never noticed?"

"We were oblivious until she became pregnant. Darcy guessed and caught them on Earth."

Danny Loco glared at him.

"We summoned a court hearing and your mother confessed to everything. Because of her position on the Council, we let her decide her own punishment."

Hi Brid took a drink of water.

"She chose to banish herself from the Maya Council, terminate her relationship with Julius Webb, and to give him—and herself—the Missing Memory potion so they would forget each other forever.

"The Council approved the punishment and erased the memory in everyone except myself and Darcy, in case we needed it in the future."

"My life's a lie." Danny Loco shook his head. "My mother's a criminal."

"Not a lie," Hi Brid said. "We've just kept an indiscretion of your mother's from you. You didn't need to know. She's not a criminal."

"You decide what's necessary for me to know about *my* history? *My* mother? As for you—" Danny Loco pointed at Cool T. "How long have you known?"

"I understand you're angry," Hi Brid said.

"*Do you?*" Danny Loco spat across the room.

Hi Brid looked at him. "That's not all."

Danny Loco waited.

"Your father is Julius Webb."

"What! That *psychopath?*" Danny Loco sprung to his feet. "Does he know?"

"We don't think he took all the potion. His memory may have returned."

"Who knows all this?" Danny Loco asked.

"All the council members have been notified," Hi Brid said.

"Everyone *except* me?" Danny Loco said.

"I wanted you focused on an antidote."

"Stuff you. You're on your own, Hi Brid." And Danny Loco stormed out of the Assembly Room.

Joy sat at the computer in Danny Loco's lab. She entered Teal's symptoms and began a search for possible remedies. The first ten hits said, 'No remedy available.' She gulped. She had to help Teal. She was the first trainee Switcher who thanked Joy when she cooked in the Switcher Centre.

They'd become friends, swapped recipes over a few milkshakes at the Open-Air Café, and had each other in stitches with kitchen disaster stories.

Joy knew Teal would be chosen amongst the latest trainees—such talent—but this, and on her first switch? So young. She shook her head. A tear rolled down her cheek.

The eleventh hit appeared on the screen, success prediction only ten per cent. She wondered. She would have to run across half of Joya to get the ingredients. There was one she didn't have, but she had an idea.

She wiped her face and shot out of the laboratory.

Darcy sat on a sofa at Prince George's place. Teal lay on the other sofa, her breathing slight, eyes closed. Zeus reached up from the floor and held her paw.

"A great Switcher." Zeus put his face in his hands.

Darcy nodded. "She had talent. And spirit."

Tears trickled down Darcy's snout. She could hear Teal's voice in her mind, *"I can do it, Darcy, honest I can."* Darcy shook her head. She had made a mistake twelve years ago, snuck her best friend down to see Earth. She could still hear the ring of the shotgun. And now here she sat with her best friend's daughter, who she'd also brought to her death.

She would tear Julius apart.

Julius tied the poodle up and threw a bucket of water over her to bring her around.

She blinked, then opened her eyes wide.

Julius smiled. "Darcy?"

She said nothing.

He poured a drop of acid on her right paw, and she screamed out.

"Tell me."

She squirmed at her paw, then looked up at the wire trailing down the left side of her face.

"A lie detector," Julius said.

He leaned toward her.

"Darcy?"

She shook her head. He clenched his fists. What did he have to *do*?

"Who are you?"

"Lickety Split Maya."

Julius raised his eyebrows. "A Dyad, eh? A *pure* Maya."

Lickety Split started shaking.

"Yes, know a lot, don't I? I want Darcy to suffer, like I have." He pushed his palm into his forehead. "I hate her."

Lickety Split shuddered. She watched the flesh peel away on her paw.

Julius had no choice. He would have to blow a hole through the connection. He'd tried everything else.

"Give me the coordinates of the oxygen/nitrogen connection."

Lickety Split closed her eyes, shook her head.

He threatened her with hot pokers and pliers to pull out her nails. She said nothing.

"I *will* get Darcy down here."

Lickety Split winced.

He grabbed her left paw, and she flinched. He pulled out a nail with the pliers. Lickety Split screamed. Tears streamed down her snout.

"Thanks for your support there, Cool T," Hi Brid said.

"What could *I* do?"

Hi Brid buried his face in his hands.

The Magi Screen buzzed purple light.

Freddie screamed down the Magi Pod. "We've got a problem, man. I need help, NOW!"

"What is it, Freddie?" Hi Brid said.

"Malcolm's collapsed, floatin´ in and out of consciousness. Must of taken on some of the illness when he switched."

Hi Brid closed his eyes. Not Malcolm.

"We've lost Danny Loco," Hi Brid said. "He's gone walkabout."

"What? Who the hell's making the antidote, then?"

Hi Brid and Cool T looked at each other.

"Get an antidote down here, *now*, or switch us back. I don't know, do *something,* man!"

The connection closed.

"Find Danny Loco," Hi Brid said. Cool T left the Assembly Room.

Freddie flew about the drawing room in 11 Downing Street. Dictionary Boy burst in. Freddie perched himself on the back of a chair.

"Spill. Spill," he said.

The words raced out of Dictionary Boy.

"He's there. At his house. Julius Webb. He's got Lickety Split. Knocked her unconscious, grabbed me. I bit him. Ran through the window. I left her behind. I don't believe it—I left her behind."

Freddie flapped his wings. "Did you have your Magi Pod?"

"No. Why?"

"Hold still." Freddie pecked a bit of glass out of Dictionary Boy's face and dropped it on the table.

"Teal won't last the hour," Freddie said. "Malcolm's in a coma."

"No." Dictionary Boy looked to the ceiling, blinked. "Not Malcolm."

"I'm guessin' Hi Brid's spilled," Freddie said, "'cause Loco's done a runner, so we've got no antidote."

"What are we going to do? Freddie, what have I done? I left Lickety Split there."

"What choice did you have, man? If you'd stayed he'd have two captives and no one would know to come save you."

"I should've done something."

"Come on," Freddie said. "Ain't nothing I can do for Malcolm, man. Let's hope there's an antidote at Julius's house. We'll update everyone on the way. Grab my Magi Pod. I'll hide in your jacket."

Chapter 16

Jon reached level four on PowerSword, then crashed. He couldn't concentrate; the empty Blib in its cradle taunted him. Why hadn't Teal sent a message? He looked up at the Funky Fountain, watched the multi-coloured water cascade down the mountain. He sighed and put the laptop on the stone armchair next to him.

He heard a whoosh overhead and watched Danny Loco land his rocket. He stomped towards the fountain, head down, hands stuffed in the pockets of his white lab coat.

"Hey!" Jon said.

Danny Loco flopped into an armchair. Jon walked over and sat next to him.

"How you doing?" Jon asked.

"Been better."

"Share it if you like," Jon said.

"What?" Danny Loco glared at him.

"What's up?" Jon said. "Let me help you."

"Huh. What could *you* do?"

"Okay, forget it." Jon jumped up from the chair and walked away. He had enough to worry about with Teal.

Wait!" Danny Loco said.

Jon turned.

"You won't believe it, but here goes—my dad isn't dead."

"That's great."

"*No*. He's an Earthie."

"Thanks a lot."

"There are rules. It's the worst crime up here."

"Why?"

"It just is, okay? And he's a maniac. He's made this deadly virus; Teal's dying from it, they—"

"What!?" Jon felt sick. "What are you doing?"

"Nothing. Why should I?"

"Are you crazy? Teal's dying. Help her! You can find a cure."

Danny Loco shrugged. "I've tried."

Jon should have followed his instincts, warned Teal. He took a deep breath, ran a hand through his hair.

"Danny, please. If anyone can help her, you can."

"I've always thought of Hi Brid as my … A dad wouldn't keep that information."

Jon placed a hand on his friend's shoulder.

"Parents are just people with a title, remember? They make mistakes."

Danny Loco stared at him.

"Please," Jon said. "Help her."

Hobo ran over.

"Why's your Magi Pod off? I don't care if you've fallen out with Hi Brid—Malcolm's collapsed."

"What?!" Jon and Danny Loco yelled at the same time.

Danny looked up at the fountain. "Tell me what to do," he said.

The multi-coloured water bubbled from the top of the fountain, erupted, and soaked the three of them. A Native American Indian hovered above it. Three blue feathers adorned his silky black hair. He wore buckskin trousers, his chest and feet bare.

"If you'd kept your mind open, you would have heard me," the Indian said.

Danny nodded.

"It's time for the Toxin Tonic." The Indian looked at Jon then back to Danny Loco. "You know what to do."

The Indian dissolved into the fountain.

Danny Loco glanced at Jon, then took a pen and paper from his coat pocket and wrote a list. He gave it to Hobo.

"Go to the far side of the planet," he said. "Take two branches from the Rigorous Tree—no need to tell you to be polite. Get those ferrets over there to help you with the rest of the list." Hobo nodded and went.

"I need something of yours, Jon," Danny Loco said. "Are you up for it?"

"Anything, if it saves Teal and Malcolm."

Danny Loco slapped him on the back. "Good man. I'll explain on the way."

Jon had a thought. "Is anyone feeding Teal?"

"What?"

"Rabbits need constant food. They're the only animal you don't starve before an operation."

"Even Maya rabbits?"

"She's in an Earthie body right now, isn't she?"

"Come on," Danny Loco said. He grabbed Jon by the T-shirt. They flew back to the castle and dumped the rocket outside. Danny ran to his lab and Jon went to the Assembly Room.

When Danny Loco walked into his lab he heard his mum crying before he saw her. She sat on the floor surrounded by plant extracts, including two branches from the Rigorous Tree.

"Mum, the antidote, you got it figured."

"It's no good," his mum said. "We need the blood of a human boxer. I thought I could cheat—mix Rocket Ron's blood with the chancellor's—but it won't work."

221

Danny Loco put his arm around her. "No problem, Mum. Jon's offered his blood."

"Jon?" Joy said. "He's not a boxer."

"Yes, he is. I've seen him. He's a natural, and Blue Feathers confirmed it."

Jon walked into the Assembly Room. Hi Brid paced up and down, muttering to himself. His wolf sat on a blue cushion nearby.

"Hh, hm," Jon said.

Hi Brid looked up.

"Teal needs food," Jon said.

"What?"

Jon shared his knowledge about rabbits.

"I think it's too late for her," Hi Brid said.

Jon wanted to scream.

Hi Brid turned to his wolf. Neither opened their mouths, but after a few moments Hi Brid nodded to the wolf and spoke to the Magi Screen.

He told Darcy to set up a drip, closed the connection, and his brown-black eyes narrowed at Jon.

"Where's Danny Loco?"

Cool T walked into the room. "Working on the antidote. He wants you, Jon."

Jon nodded and left the room as the Magi Screen buzzed purple light.

Agent Shatner woke up and cursed himself. Julius could've walked right past him. He stuffed half an energy bar in his mouth, got out of the car, and raced to the front door. He picked the lock and sneaked through the house to the lab.

Julius ran out of the back door with a fire extinguisher in his arms. Shatner stood in something sticky and looked down at a pool of blood. He looked across the lab and saw a black poodle, unconscious. He guessed the blood on the floor came from the dog. What on earth …

Shatner ran out the back door to see Julius speed down the garden, past the open gates, and into the park on his quad bike.

The truth potion had to be in that fire extinguisher. Shatner ran back through the house. He jumped into his car and pressed the tracker receiver: Nothing.

"No!" he screamed.

He touched every button: still nothing. He pulled the receiver off the dash and shook it. The screen flashed, then faded.

Hi Brid looked up as Joy entered the Assembly Room.

"Are you okay?" Joy said.

Hi Brid shook his head. "Lickety Split's been captured."

Joy gasped.

"Cool T's flipped," Hi Brid said. "He's gone down there without switching with a Trader, Darcy won't leave Teal, we've got the two stand-ins at Jon's house. It's a mess. With this imbalance, we're looking at an earthquake within the hour."

"I've got some good news," Joy said.

"The antidote?"

Joy nodded. "I've just come from the hospital. I've given the chancellor a shot. He's responding."

Danny Loco and Jon burst into the room.

"We're going to Earth," Danny Loco said.

"No way, not until I get someone back here," Hi Brid said. "Cool T's already gone."

Hi Brid yelled after them, but they ignored him.

Chapter 17

Freddie sat on Dictionary Boy's shoulder outside Julius Webb's house. Cool T walked up behind them.

"Hi, guys," Cool T said.

Dictionary Boy and Freddie jumped out of their skin and feathers.

"You crazy, man? You could've given a parrot a heart attack. A heart attack."

"I couldn't sit around on Joya. An extra bit of muscle won't hurt with this lunatic."

"Aren't you going to cause an imbalance?" Freddie said, brushing his feathers back down.

"Better be quick, then," Cool T said.

They went through the house to the lab. They could smell burning flesh.

Lickety Split had been tied up and attached to a machine, blood all around her. She had a nail missing from one paw, the other one burnt and blistered. She didn't seem to be breathing. Cool T went over to her. Nothing. He started pumping her chest.

He continued for a few minutes, then stopped.

"My little girl," he said. He shook his head, closed his eyes. "She's gone."

"No!" Dictionary Boy said. "It's my fault. I left her." He threw himself on top of Lickety Split, punched his fists into her chest.

Cool T pulled him off and held him until he stopped punching. Freddie looked up at the ceiling to keep the tears away.

Lickety Split coughed. Freddie flew to her.

She opened her eyes.

"She's in a trance, man."

Cool T wiped his eyes.

"She's so deep. So deep," Freddie said.

Cool T made an emergency transmission to Hobo. No connection. He tried Darcy. Nothing.

He rubbed his forehead with his hand. "The Magi Pod connection's dead."

Freddie saw a note pinned to the back of Lickety Split's chair. He grabbed it in his beak and handed it to Cool T.

By the time you read this, Maya filth, it will be too late, for her, and for all of you. I crushed both paws and she still wouldn't talk, but hypnotism she couldn't fight. She gave me the coordinates of your connection, and I'll blast a hole right through it. Without the connection, you die.

Cool T balled up the note and clenched his teeth.

"He's a spangle short of sanity, man," Freddie said.

Cool T untied Lickety Split.

"You two get back to Malcolm," he said. "Better he isn't alone." He draped Lickety Split in his arms. He looked down at her, his voice breaking. "I'll go to Darcy. She needs to know. Go."

Joya started to shudder and shift under them. Hi Brid fell, his wolf jumping out of the way just in time.

Joy looked at Hi Brid. "The Earth connection's been broken."

Hi Brid picked himself up. "Lickety Split must have given the coordinates."

"We haven't been hit full on, or we'd be dead," Joy said. "Although, this could just be the start."

"Comforting," Hi Brid said. "We've got to get back in range fast—or we lose everyone."

"Danny's got a reactor in his lab," Joy said, "to boost us out of trouble or bring us closer if we fall out of range. It's never been used because, well, because this has never happened. It might not work, even."

"Get in that lab and *make* it work!" Hi Brid said.

Cool T arrived at Prince George's place, Lickety Split in his arms. Teal had a makeshift drip in her arm. Zeus covered her with a sheet.

A lump the size of a mountain grew in Cool T′s throat. It took all his strength to keep standing. She'd been a fine rabbit.

Darcy looked up. "Is Lickety Split—"

"No. She's in a trance. Help her, Darcy, please." Cool T placed Lickety Split on an armchair and crumpled. His tears fell on her fur.

Darcy walked over, looked into Lickety Split's eyes, and shook her head.

"She's too deep. Only Hobo can help her."

Cool T explained about the note and the Magi Pod problem.

Darcy closed her eyes. "So he's done it," she said.

Hobo led Prince George and his rabbit into the Assembly Room. Hi Brid stopped pacing and exhaled. "We have a problem—our oxygen/nitrogen connection's been severed. It also serves as our transport line, so—"

The planet shook. Hi Brid and Hobo fell to the floor. Prince George and his rabbit fell backwards and crashed into the doors.

The four doctors in the Maya hospital all looked at each other. The chancellor asked what had happened. They didn't know.

They roped the chancellor into the bed for his own safety and sat around on the floor holding onto the bed.

The only other patient, a giraffe with whiplash, had laid himself on the floor after falling out of bed during the first quake. He cried out as the shudders jolted through his neck. One of the doctors crawled along the floor to give him some Reiki.

Jon and Danny Loco flew down the transport line on Danny's rocket. They stopped three metres above Earth and turned left.

They heard a quad bike and looked back. A man in a gas mask jumped off the quad, picked up a fire extinguisher, and started to spray the connection.

"NOOOO!" Danny Loco screamed.

He turned the rocket and flew straight for the man.

The man looked up at the rocket. He pulled off the gas mask.

"Arabella!" he shouted.

Jon noticed Danny Loco flinch in front of him.

Jon jumped off the rocket and dived onto the man, knocking the fire extinguisher out of his hands and winding him as his knees landed on the man's stomach. He stared at the older version of Danny Loco. The man went for Jon's throat, but Jon blocked him and threw a right hook for Teal. Saliva flew out of the man's mouth as his head jerked to the side.

Jon started to choke on the fumes and covered his mouth.

Danny Loco landed the rocket and ran over. He picked up the gas mask, put it on Jon, and looked down at Julius. His mouth dropped open. His father stared back at him. Danny Loco lifted his lab coat to cover his mouth.

"Son." Julius coughed. "The lab coat, a scientist like me." He spluttered. A tear rolled down his cheek. "Get away," he managed to croak, as the mixture from the fire extinguisher filled his lungs. He managed a smile, then closed his eyes.

Danny Loco started coughing into his coat.

Jon ripped off the gas mask and put it on Danny Loco.

"Come on! Teal and Malcolm need us." Jon dragged Danny back to the rocket.

Agent Shatner arrived on the scene to find Julius Webb unconscious next to the canister, his quad bike nearby. He didn't want to get out of the car. The canister could be dangerous. He called the emergency services and his friend Chief Burns. Let them check it out first. But that extinguisher belonged to him.

Joy broke the emergency box containing three liquids and poured them into the reactor. She set the coordinates for a certain place in England, and waited.

231

Jon and Danny Loco rushed into Prince George's. Cool T took the gas mask off Danny Loco. Jon had the mother of all headaches. He looked over at a black poodle flopped on an armchair, then noticed the sheet on the sofa. Teal's left ear poked out from under it. No!

He ripped the sheet from Teal's body. Danny Loco gave her a dose of the antidote. Jon listened for a heart beat. Nothing.

"Give her another one," Jon said. Danny Loco looked at him.

"Go on!" Jon said.

He did. Jon saw the drip still had food going into Teal. She didn't move. He couldn't feel a pulse. He clutched her paw, swallowed.

Danny Loco turned to Darcy and Zeus, told them what had happened with Julius. Cool T explained about Lickety Split.

Jon looked across at the poodle—he felt sick. Not Lickety Split, too.

"He did it to get the coordinates," Zeus said.

Danny Loco shook his head. "I can't believe that man we just saw is the monster who tortured Lickety Split. Can't believe he's my dad."

"*We* created the monster," Darcy said.

Danny Loco looked at Darcy.

Teal's chest rose and fell.

"Look!" Jon cried.

Everyone turned.

Jon put his finger on Teal's neck and felt the pulse getting stronger. The double dose of antidote had restarted her heart.

"What about Malcolm?" Zeus said.

Danny Loco looked at Jon. "Come on."

The two of them shot out of the door.

The speed Joya travelled caused everyone on the planet to feel dizzy or nauseous.

The doctors in the hospital watched the chancellor's face turn green, and fought to untie themselves from his bed.

The giraffe flew across the floor and hit his head on the iron leg of one of the beds.

The wavy table in the Assembly Room had uprooted and crashed into pieces. The cushions had become a makeshift multi-coloured mountain in one corner of the room.

Chapter 18

Jon and Danny Loco hovered outside the back of 11 Downing Street. They looked through the upper window. Freddie and Dictionary Boy sat on the bed, Malcolm lay under the covers. Dictionary Boy jumped up to let them in.

Jon ran over to Malcolm and searched for a pulse. Nothing.

Danny Loco gave Malcolm a double dose of the antidote. He winked at Jon. "Worked with Teal."

They waited and checked his pulse again. Nothing. Danny Loco shook his head. They looked at each other. Not Malcolm. Danny Loco stepped away. Jon ran a hand through his hair, swallowed the rock wedged in his throat.

Malcolm opened his eyes and groaned. Freddie flapped around like a crazy bird. Dictionary Boy slid off the bed.

Freddie's Magi Pod buzzed purple light.

Hi Brid's voice wavered. "*Please* tell me we're not too late, that some of you are all right down there."

Danny Loco grabbed the Magi Pod from the bed.

"Hi Brid," he said. "We're all fine. Malcolm and Teal have come round. Lickety Split's in a deep trance. We need Hobo."

"On his way," Hi Brid said. "Can you and Jon get back here, before we cause an earthquake down there? Tell Cool T I can't send Hobo till he comes back."

"Sure thing—Dad."

Freddie and Dictionary Boy stared at Danny Loco. He ignored them. Jon smiled at his friend.

Danny Loco gave Jon a leg up on to the rocket, and they flew off to get Cool T and tell Darcy and Zeus the good news.

Hi Brid wiped his eyes with the back of his hand. They hadn't lost a Switcher. And Danny Loco had called him *Dad*.

He looked up to see Hobo smiling at him.

"*What?*" he said. "Don't you have somewhere you should be?"

Hobo saluted and left.

Joy walked into the Assembly Room, bits of sick in her hair.

"We have *you* to thank for this, do we?" Hi Brid gestured around the room.

"Afraid so," Joy said. "I had no idea what would happen, really."

"Oh, well, that's reassuring."

Joy smiled. "Thank goodness we raised such a great scientist. If Danny hadn't made that reactor, none of us would … we would all be … well, you know."

Hi Brid nodded. Yes, he knew. His heart burst with pride and relief.

Hobo arrived on Earth and worked his brilliance with Lickety Split. It took two hours to bring her out of her trance. She couldn't talk about the torture.

Luckily for Joya, Lickety Split always muddled her numbers. She'd given Julius what she *thought* were the right coordinates. Julius believed her because the lie detector confirmed her honesty. It meant that he aimed his extinguisher a little too far to the left, so instead of pushing Joya light years away, it had only travelled half a day.

Hobo bandaged Lickety Split's paws. Darcy and Zeus grimaced at the state of them. Lickety Split had a desire to lick them but cringed at the thought.

"It's the penicillin in your saliva," Hobo said. "All dogs have it. You want to repair yourself."

"No, Hobo. What I want is to *never* be a dog again. No offense, Darcy."

Darcy smiled. "None taken."

"We don't know if Julius Webb is dead," Zeus said.

"My thoughts exactly," Darcy said. "If you'll excuse me."

Before they returned to Earth, Joy gave the prime minister, the chancellor, and their pets shots of both the Missing Memory potion and the Toxin Tonic.

Prince George returned to Earth, gave his grandmother the Toxin Tonic in a cup of tea, and slipped some into Lancelot's milk. Hi Brid asked him to stay and make sure they drank it all. Even though the queen hadn't seemed to contract the virus, Hi Brid wanted to be sure.

That night, while Prince George slept, Cool T snuck in and gave the prince and his rabbit the Missing Memory potion.

The stand-ins at Jon's house agreed to stay for the rest of Jon and Jen's six weeks so Zeus could return and get some well-earned rest. They reported Teal's first assignment a success: Mr Neville Parker now spent hours every day with his horse Hector—who, somehow, had learned to smile.

The hospital didn't have a bed free. Jon and Danny Loco had to stay in for an hour to flush out the toxins from the fire extinguisher. A green liquid went in one tube and a murky brown sludge came out another.

Lickety Split's hands didn't look great. She had to stay in for a few more days to have skin grafts and bone rebuilding. She also had a few bruised ribs where Dictionary Boy had punched her.

He'd sent bright pink sunflowers, which stood tall in a vase beside her bed, and a note with ten different ways to say sorry.

Malcolm would be released tomorrow and had been told off for using his bed as a trampoline.

Teal laughed at his jokes but she still felt weak and wouldn't be leaving the hospital for a few days. Jon and Danny Loco hadn't stopped talking to each other since they arrived, so Teal didn't get the chance to say thank you to Jon. He had saved her life. She would do something special for him when she got out of hospital.

Teal looked towards the door and saw her dad. A hand tugged at her heart, a Maya boulder in her throat. He walked up to the bed, sat back on his haunches, and shook his head.

Tears welled up in Teal's eyes.

"Dad, I'm ..."

Her dad leaned down and hugged her tight. They cried an Unfathomable Lake between them.

Darcy had remained on Earth to deal with Julius Webb. As she approached the old connection point, she saw three police cars and an ambulance. Darcy couldn't risk going any closer, but if Julius had survived she would sniff him out if it took her a lifetime.

Jon and Danny Loco walked into the Assembly Room and sank onto the giant cushions. Hi Brid, Freddie, and Cool T all cheered. The two heroes beamed at each other.

"You saved Teal's life, Jon," Hi Brid said. "And I hear your newly acquired boxing skills prevented a more severed connection."

Jon grinned at Danny Loco. "Teamwork," he said.

Hi Brid put a hand on Danny Loco's shoulder. "Are you all right?"

"Yes and no. On the one hand, I've found out about my father. On the other—"

"He ain't such a great guy?" Freddie stretched out, and placed his paws behind his head.

Danny Loco scowled at him. "No. On the other hand, I feel like my whole life's been a lie. For the first time, I feel a bit stupid."

Everyone looked at him.

"You all knew I had an Earthie for a father, a few of you knew all my life. I feel a bit out of the loop, know what I mean?"

"Secrets happen sometimes, man," Freddie said, half to himself. "We survive."

Danny Loco leaned towards Freddie.

"Get out of it, man." Freddie raised a paw at Danny Loco. "Keep outta my mind."

"Hell, let's hope we don't have any of our *other* secrets exposed," Cool T said.

All eyes went to him. They all shouted at once.

"What other secrets?!"

Acknowledgements

Huge thanks to Renni Browne for your wonderful belief and support, showing me what I'm capable of, turning this book into what it is, ripping me out of my skin to show me what I could do out of my comfort zone, and showing me the joys of editing and the secret wonders of line editing.

Thanks to Rabbit Secrets by Maitland Sinclair and Kelly Bird, ARBA Registrar, for answering my rabbit questions.

Big thanks to Rita Newing for editing the early draft.

Thank you to Nadine, Debbie, Jo and Matt for well needed help and advice.

Thanks to Rosa Martinez for the most incredible experience on a motorbike. Gracias, guapetona.

Big thanks to boxing trainer, Patrick Kelly, for two years training.

Thanks to Kathryn Robinson, Helen Corner and Lee Weatherly at Cornerstones for teaching me so much.

A million thank yous to actress Silvia Galve Marti for unbelievable support and belief. I wish I could give all authors a friend like you. Gracias, mi amor.

Thank you, Tricia Essery, for believing in this book from the start and believing in me.

And Gwyneth, Tom and Harry Ashcroft what can I say? Your belief and support and enthusiasm and feedback have filled my heart. Thank you.

Thank you to all my family and friends who have believed in me and finally get to read the book.

To God and the angels, thank you for giving me such a fun story to write and so much more.

Thank you to YouWriteOn.com for this wonderful opportunity.

And my giant thanks go to my husband, Lee. Thank you so much for putting up with me while my body was on Earth but my mind refused to leave the fun of Joya, staying up late giggling about Freddie and co., supporting me, superb editing and having to read this book in all its versions so many times. You rock.

Want to know more about the
characters and the author?

Check out ...

<u>www.lianecarter.com</u>

Printed in the United Kingdom by
Lightning Source UK Ltd., Milton Keynes
142210UK00002BA/2/P